Pressed to the Nines

The Charmed Inn Mysteries, Book 4
Misty Simon

This is a work of fiction. Names, characters, places, and incidents either are the product of the author's imagination or are used fictitiously, and any resemblance to actual persons living or dead, business establishments, events, or locales, is entirely coincidental.

© COPYRIGHT 2026 by Misty Simon

All rights reserved. No part of this book may be used or reproduced in any manner whatsoever without written permission of the publisher except in the case of brief quotations embodied in critical articles or reviews.

AI was not used to write this book, to create the cover art, or in formatting.

NO AI TRAINING: Without in any way limiting the author's and publisher's exclusive rights under copyright, any use of this publication to "train" generative artificial intelligence (AI) technologies to generate text is expressly prohibited. The author reserves all rights to license uses of this work for genAI training and development of machine learning language models.

Warning: Not intended for persons under the age of 18. May contain coarse language and mature content that may disturb some readers. Reader discretion advised.

Cover Art Design by: Kelly Moran/Rowan Prose Publishing
Photo Credit: Adobe Images/Deposit Photos
First Edition
ISBN: 978-1-971276-07-6
Rowan Prose Publishing, LLC
www.RowanProsePublishing.com
Published in the United States of America

Get the other books in the series now!

PRAISE FOR MISTY SIMON:

"Cozy fans will be charmed."
-Publishers Weekly

"A mystery like no other I have read."
-Lisa K's Reviews Blog

"You'll be cheering as the clues pile up in this creative cozy mystery."
-Lynn Cahoon, *New York Times* bestselling author

"A down-to-earth heroine."
-Kirkus Reviews

"An amusing new series with an engaging, spirited sleuth."
-Library Journal

"A cast of entertaining characters."
-Kings River Life Magazine

"Simon has you laughing out loud."
-Cozy Mystery Book Reviews

Chapter 1

Why was it so hard to train a cat to walk on a leash? That seemed to be the question of the day. Although, to be fair to my little feline, Mustafa, who I affectionately called Moose, he was almost thirteen and had never been outside, much less on a leash. So, I was asking a lot of him, and I knew it. But I really wanted him to be my ring bearer in my long-anticipated wedding to the most delicious of men, one Dean Manchester.

And that meant training Moose to walk on a leash, because there was absolutely no way he would walk down the aisle under his own steam without running amok. It wasn't a short walk, but it was completely out of the realm of possibility that he would peacefully stroll out of the house, into the backyard, and then down a runner to the gazebo, currently draped in antique string lights.

"Moose, baby, lovey, feline of my heart, I need you to walk." I'd admit that I sounded desperate, and that was because I very much *was* desperate for this to go off without a hitch. No one needed to tell me it was only one day. And I'd often thought that if it was the best day of my life, then that meant I had a long way to go without being able to top it. I was anticipating many more even, better days in the years to come. But right now, I wanted it to be the very best day of my life—up to this point.

Part of that day included my adorable, but lazy, cat unfurling himself from the ground and walking along on the leash so that he could deliver our rings to us. Isaac, Dean's nephew, had agreed to lead the cat down the aisle, followed closely by Dean's niece, Amelia, who would be throwing the flower petals.

Well, not throwing. We did have to have a talk about that early on. She had thought perhaps she could chuck them at those whom she wanted to pelt with missiles. After much discussion, we got her to agree to only do that in her imagination as she gently dropped the hundreds of sunflower and peony petals on her way to the arch Dean and his brother, Caper, had added to the gazebo.

I absolutely adored the beautiful piece they had worked so hard on. Not just for the beauty of it, but for the blood, sweat, tears—and lots of swearing—that had gone into it. The arch was made from a solid chunk of sequoia Dean had sourced from someone on the West Coast. It was carved exquisitely with books, tools, and Celtic knots. Our first names were tooled right in the middle. The guys had made the whole thing with some help from a man in town who was a master carver.

Dean had taken months studying how to carve, almost an apprenticeship under Bob Melton, to be able to put silhouettes of both of us surrounded by all the people who meant so much to us, both living and not. It was a reflection of the oak library door that my long ago, and far away, great times seven or so, grandfather had carved when he began his life with my ancestor, Mary Margaret.

And when we were done with it here, after we decompressed from all the hoopla, it would be moved to sit above the doorway into my two-story library inside the inn I owned. I couldn't wait! For both the day after this wedding and to have the arch up.

It wasn't that I wanted the wedding to be over. I just wanted the stress of the wedding to be over, as well as the planning, and the trying to fulfill certain people's wishes, but not losing the essence of what Dean and I wanted for our big day.

I'd even hired a wedding planner to take over most of the smaller details, like getting things set up for the outdoor wedding. She'd done a pretty good job so far and had taken loads off my mind while I did my real job, managing the inn.

To be honest, though, I just wanted to be able to say, "I do," and get it over with. The journey after that was what it was all about, not the hokey pokey this decorating thing felt like it was turning into. No wonder some people went to the Justice of the Peace over at the courthouse and then just had a big celebration afterwards.

If I could go back to last year when I said yes to Dean's proposal to make our life together, and the handfasting we did under the full moon with our small families present, I would have totally put in my vote for a small ceremony instead of this big one. Although I probably would have been shot down right from the start because Dean wanted a big shindig. I would gladly give him anything, even this mess of a big day. Including Moose walking our rings down the aisle.

"Come on, Moose. I need you to at least kind of pretend that you're going to do this thing."

But the cat continued to lie on his side. If I hadn't been able to see his chest moving, I would have perhaps thought he had left this world to go chase dust bunnies in the sky. His chest did move, though, and so did his eyes, as he stared at me, then slowly blinked and turned his head away.

"Trouble?" my beloved asked, coming up alongside me.

"Always," I answered, rolling my eyes.

"Mustafa, we'd like you to be a part of this wedding," Dean said. "If you'd rather not, then we can make an exception and bring in the puppy Caper just got from the animal rescue. Your choice, buddy."

And did that get him right up and swaying his way down the exact path I had been carrying him up and down for the last three days? Yes, yes, it did.

"Jerk," I mumbled under my breath. "Not you," I said louder, turning to Dean.

"I knew that wasn't directed at me, but as long as he's doing the thing, we shouldn't care why. Are you okay with that?"

I grumbled a bit, but ultimately agreed and then admired the casual stroll Moose was doing, crossing his legs in the front like he was on some kind of catwalk in a huge fashion show. Then I harrumphed anyway. "He should have done it because I asked him to."

"And yet he's doing it now. Let's just hope he does the same on the actual day. If not, we could always try to talk Isaac into carrying the cat down the aisle, if it's that important to you." Dean kissed me on the forehead and then on the lips when I tipped my chin up to look into his eyes. Those gray eyes twinkled right before he closed them, and that made everything right as I sank into enjoying his lips on mine.

When he pulled back, I felt the loss, but it was probably for the best. Amelia had come tearing out of the house with the puppy Dean had mentioned, hot on her heels. The girl laughed, and the dog barked, and the cat jumped high enough to be caught in mid-air by Dean without him having to bend over.

Moose climbed farther up Dean's chest to drape himself around Dean's neck on his shoulders. Poor baby. Both of them. As soon as the puppy saw Dean, she started bouncing off his leg. Because she was a dachshund, she only made it above his ankle, but still.

"Oof." He nearly bobbled Moose with the impact. Daffy Daffodil, the dachshund, might have been tiny, but she was extremely powerful with that pounce.

I couldn't help it, I giggled.

"Roxy Gleason, soon to be Winchester, this is not a laughing matter," he said sternly, or at least, he tried to sound stern, but he totally missed the point.

Ah, yes, I was still working on remembering that he had decided to go back to using his actual last name, instead of hiding behind the fake Manchester he'd used for years to distance himself from his family and their reputation. And yes, that did make him Dean Winchester again, for those *Supernatural* fans, which he still had to make peace with, but we were working on it.

"Amelia, why don't you grab Daffy and take her for a walk?" I said. "We're due to start the rehearsal in about an hour, and then we'll be having dinner. Getting her out for her walk now might be your best bet."

The girl smiled at me, and my heart felt like it was glowing right in my chest. I had never really thought about having anything more than the inn I'd dreamed of since I was five years old. As far as the future went, it had just involved hosting travelers, families, and groups, until I was too old to take care of things anymore, which would have been about sixty years from now.

But then, Dean had entered my life, bringing with him a niece and nephew I cared deeply about, a brother I adored, and a future I had never considered, but now did not want to live any other way.

My cell phone vibrated in my pocket. I wasn't expecting any calls, but since it was the day before the wedding, I couldn't ignore anything right now.

I answered as soon as I saw it was Sharon, the wedding planner I'd hired a few months ago to help me. She was new to town and had been recommended by the florist as a top-notch planner. I hoped that held true for whatever she was calling about now.

"Hey, Sharon." I gave my best cheerful inn owner voice.

"Roxy! You sound happy!"

Despite the exclamation points in her voice, I had a sinking feeling in my stomach. Was she also putting on the fake charm? "Just finishing up some last-minute things before we start rehearsal. You're going to be here for that, right?"

"Sure, yes, of course. But listen, Emma over at Petal Paradise just called."

My heart sank into the Converse on my feet. I was expecting a delivery in thirty minutes. Please don't let them run into a snag. Please!

"Don't worry, we still have your flowers," she said quickly. "They're all ready to go, but their driver is having some car issues, and Rick is stuck out at the campground. Emma said she's at the shop for a little bit longer. Is there any way you could pick up the flowers? I'll get them to refund you the delivery fee. Sorry about this."

I quietly released the breath I had been holding and smiled for real. "No problem at all. I can go now."

"That would be awesome. Emma said she'll wait to help Rick at the campground until you get there. If the door's locked, though, let me know, and I can get it open for you. Sorry again for the inconvenience. Stupid cars."

My laughter was not in any way forced, which felt wonderful. "I feel that in my soul. There's no need to apologize or worry. I have no problem running over to the store and getting the bouquets now. On my way."

"So appreciated! Let me know when you have them, and I'll check them off my many lists."

We said our goodbyes after I thanked her again and said I wished the driver well with his transportation issues, and then I turned to Dean. "I'm going to go grab the flowers. Car troubles, and Rick is stuck at the campground."

"Do you want me to go with you?"

I reached up to pat his cheek. "I've got this, but thanks. You stay here and see if you can get Moose to do his walk again, just to make sure it wasn't a fluke."

"Okay, be careful. I want to see you at that arch tonight and definitely tomorrow."

"Always." And the idea of tomorrow made my heart sparkle like the pages of the books I talked to as a bibliomancer, my talent that allowed me to ask questions and then read a passage of a book and get the answer. It didn't always work, even now, but it worked more often than not, and I appreciated that. Plus, I'd been able to get those books to sparkle and glow more consistently over the last several months when asking questions about life stuff instead of only glowing when the answers involved murder. It was a lovely thing to do, and I'd been working with my Aunt Hellen and Uncle Vince, while they were also teaching Amelia about her talent as an aeromancer, someone who could work with the atmosphere.

But all *mancy* stuff had been put on hold for the next week. We had a bunch of my family here, all talented in their own ways, but they'd been asked to tamp down their powers, too, because we also had a few non-talent people who were not to know what we were able to do. Maybe that would change one day in the future, but not before the end of next week. There were discussions going on at much higher levels than me about possibly coming out of the shadows for the first time in centuries, but that was not my main focus right now, with the wedding happening tomorrow.

Tomorrow! I felt like I had waited a lifetime for tomorrow.

But today, I had to get the flowers and then get right into the rehearsal and dinner. It would be a blast and also a lot of fun. For one thing, Glennis, my lovely kitchen manager, had flipped my seating chart and was going to make my sister Mena sit next to Micah Felderman. They were currently avoiding each other, or had been trying to, but Glennis had decided to make them deal with each other at dinner.

I hadn't been able to get Mena to tell me what had made them step back when they had seemed to be building something together while dating over the last year. It was on my list of things to do once the wedding was over. A lot of things seem to be on the list for after the wedding was over.

Not that I didn't want to enjoy the day, it just felt like there were so many things at stake for the big day, and I wanted to let go of the stress.

Dean caught my hand and lifted it to his mouth to kiss my knuckles, and everything faded away. He smiled and then winked at me. Of course, Moose batted at my head because he could, but even that didn't bother me in the moment.

I just wanted to be able to say "I do" to this amazing man, and then everything else would fall into place. Or, at the least, it wouldn't bother me, because we would be linked together forever on paper, as we already were in our hearts.

That should have felt schmaltzy to say, and yet it didn't.

Flowers!

"Okay, I'm headed out then. I'll be back as soon as possible, and then we do the rehearsal, then dinner, then go our separate ways one last time."

I was sticking to the plan that Dean and I would not see each other once we went to sleep until the ceremony tomorrow. It wouldn't be easy, as I had grown very accustomed to having him curled around me at night, with his arm over my waist, and him joking about how he often woke up with my hand covering his face. But tonight, I would sleep alone for the last time, and then we'd see each other at the altar in the gazebo.

I kissed him and then tore myself away to go get those bouquets I'd ordered for my two sisters, myself, my mother, and my Aunt Hellen. I'd asked for a waterfall of gardenias with tendrils of ivy for myself, and then the same for all the others, but with a pop of lilacs. If nothing else, my party was going to smell like a little slice of Heaven.

Jumping into my car, I checked all the mirrors and moved the seat, since Dean had recently been driving my family around, and always had to adjust the mechanics to fit his much bigger frame. I pulled out into traffic, humming to myself. We had a local guitarist coming tomorrow to sit in the back of the gazebo and play a bunch of music during the ceremony. He'd given us a concert in the dining room last week, and I could not wait to walk down the aisle to the lovely serenade he had prepared.

The flower shop was only on the other side of our small town on the Susquehanna River, so it didn't take long to get there. That was fortunate, since I was running up against the time Emma typically flipped the sign to "Closed" on the front door, and Rick needed help at the campground.

A bell jingled above my head as I pulled the door to me, and I entered a veritable garden of blooms, succulents, and leafy green things. It always smelled amazing in here, a potpourri of scents that teased your senses, but also left you feeling mellow, as you strolled through the small shop that was busy with so many colors and kinds of flora. Every once in a while, there was a bit of fauna in here, too, if she had Taboo in the shop, a beautiful golden retriever who was one of the most patient dogs I had ever come across. Maybe he could teach Daffy a thing or two.

As I made my way to the counter, I was surprised no one had come out of the back. Sharon had said Emma knew I was due in. Maybe I had taken a few extra minutes to say goodbye to Dean, but I wasn't that late, even with Moose being a pain. She should still be here, especially if the front door was unlocked and the sign was turned to "Open."

I tapped the bell on the front counter and waited. And waited. I tapped it again after about thirty seconds. I wasn't trying to be impatient, and if she had a customer in front of me or was showing someone around the shop, I certainly would have waited my turn, but I wasn't used to not seeing her at all.

Ringing the bell a third time, I wondered if maybe she was in the bathroom. I had heard from Aunt Hellen that Emma had been having some stomach issues lately, most likely due to a recent diagnosis. I hadn't been told what was wrong with her, and I hadn't asked, because that wasn't my business. I had, however, asked Aunt Hellen if I should move my order to another florist. Not that I had wanted to, but I didn't need to put more pressure on the woman if she was dealing with something life-threatening. But Aunt Hellen had assured me she'd be okay. Just some sickness that was being treated.

I could see the bouquets in the refrigerator behind the counter, so I should be able to grab them and skedaddle. I could let Emma know via text that I was the one who had picked them up, and I'd talk with her later. I'd already paid for them months ago when I'd first ordered them.

After ringing the bell for the fourth time, I finally heard some movement in the back. See? Maybe she had just been in the bathroom.

Unfortunately, no one came out yet, but I did hear Taboo barking toward the back. Without a second thought, I hustled around the counter and pushed the swinging door marked "Employees Only." It was a maze back here, with work benches covered in vases and boxes, ribbon and cloth. Taboo barked again, and it seemed to be coming from deeper in the shop. I pushed through another door marked private and then came to a standstill.

Taboo was barking at Emma. Emma, who was slumped against the door in what had to be a walk-in cooler with all the flowers behind her that I could see through the full glass door. But for some reason, she was leaning up against the glass with her hands placed on the door like she was trying to get out. My first inclination was to yank the door open, and I tried, but it wasn't budging. And that was when I realized her mouth was open, but there was no mist on the door in front of her to signal she was breathing. Plus, her skin had a definite blue hue to it.

This was very, very bad.

Chapter 2

I did my best to calm Taboo down. He had a leash on, so I wrapped it around the leg of a metal worktable and asked him to please stay so that I could check on Emma. I wouldn't have been able to tell you if he understood my words, but he must have at least had a clue about what I meant because he sat, still straining against the leash and whining, but he did remain sitting.

There didn't seem to be a way to open the door Emma was plastered against without having her fall out on me, so I discarded that idea as soon as I had it and just called the police. I knew enough now not to touch anything having to do with whatever had happened. And after our last murder, I had some more respect for the lead detective, Norm. He would do his best job to figure out what had happened to poor Emma. I wasn't leaning toward murder. Most likely, it was her illness that had done her in. But I wasn't taking chances, either.

I could hear the sirens about thirty seconds after I got on the line with Shirleen down at the precinct.

"Take care there, Roxy," Shirleen said. "At least it's not another murder."

"True, but still sad."

"Incredibly sad. I'll let you go so you can meet the people at the front door. Watch Taboo, he can be a runner."

After tucking my cell phone into my back pocket, I unlooped Taboo's leash from the metal counter leg and then did my best to coax him away from the glass door. "I promise someone is coming to see what happened, boy. I'm so sorry. I know she was your very favorite person in the world." I picked up my pace when I saw a group of people out on the sidewalk. The door was still unlocked, so I wasn't sure why they weren't just coming in.

But then, when I whipped the door open, or tried to, I jerked my arm so hard I felt my shoulder wrench in its socket. Ow!

Glancing down, I couldn't believe my eyes. The door was locked. How was the door locked? I'd walked in without any issues less than five minutes ago. I hadn't heard anyone come in behind me, and there had been no one in the shop besides Taboo and Emma.

All of that took about a half a second in my brain as I twisted the lock open and then swung the door wide.

"This door was not locked when it closed behind me."

Norm, the lead detective, shook his head. "Maybe the lock is broken. Let's handle the bigger emergency first."

Turning on my heel, I quickly led the four police officers and the two EMTs into the back of the shop. Taboo was not going to be left behind, and I hadn't forgotten Shirleen's warning that the dog liked to be a runner. I kept him on a tight leash with little room to wiggle as we approached the refrigerated case.

My heart broke when Taboo sat down and leaned his head against my leg, and started whining and crying softly. Poor baby. He couldn't know what was going on, and yet he did. Of course, he did. His human was no longer of this world, leaving behind just her body. He had to feel that loss.

I stroked his head as I scratched him under his chin. "They'll figure out what happened, promise."

"Did you see anything unusual when you came in, Roxy?" Norm asked in a gentle but firm tone, completely unlike how he used to talk to me, which had once been full of angst and anger.

I was so happy we were on better terms than the first time we'd met over a dead body. And thankfully, he was no longer calling me Roxanne. I didn't hate my full name, but I much preferred the nickname.

"No, I stood at the front counter for a minute or so, and then Taboo started barking back here, and I followed the noise, not sure if something had happened. I've heard that Emma was recently diagnosed with some sort of chronic disease that she was fighting, but I don't know what it was, or what kind of things she was battling."

"And you were the only one in here?" He was writing things down in his little notebook. Fortunately, I no longer felt like he was grilling me, just looking for information so he could do his best job to find out the truth.

"As far as I know. The wedding planner, Sharon, called me because they were supposed to deliver the flowers for the wedding. But the delivery driver's car was having trouble, and Rick was stuck out at the campground. So he asked Sharon to ask me to pick the flowers up. Then Emma was going to go get him and his car." Poor Richard. This would devastate him. He and Emma had been together for a whole lot of years. And he was still waiting for her to come help him at the campground.

Norm sent out a call to have someone go to Richard and break the news to him about what happened, and help him. Standing back, I watched Norm perform his duties with a professionalism I had not thought he was capable of over a year ago when he'd been working on the first murdered victim I'd stumbled across. It made me feel better about this whole situation and leaving it in his now capable hands. I didn't think it was murder, but it still was weird. Especially the circumstances with the door being locked behind me made me pause. But there had been no signs of struggle, no knives sticking out of her body, or ropes around her neck. Possibly, it was a result of a series of events, including whatever illness she had recently been diagnosed with.

Whatever it was, I left as soon as Norm told me to go.

"I know you have your wedding tomorrow. Don't worry about this. We've got it handled. I feel like I'm an old hand at this now. That doesn't exactly make me happy, but it does tell me that I won't need any assistance, especially as you have your "I do's" to do, and there's nothing here to investigate. You can take your flowers with you, too, and that box of chocolates that's marked with your name. I don't think there's any reason they can't be removed since this isn't a crime scene."

"I really appreciate that, Norm. I hope that you can get her out of the case without any problems."

"Yeah, me, too." He ran a hand over his thinning hair. I considered recommending that he go see Chessie over at her salon to figure out if there was a way to help him not lose even more hair, but now was not the time for that. Glancing at the clock on the wall, decorated with pressed flowers Emma herself had found on her daily walks, I flinched. We'd talked about that clock on one of my trips in here to discuss flowers for the inn. I'd considered doing one of my own with the flowers from the wedding as a kind of commemorative keepsake, but we'd never gotten around to discussing how to make it. And now, we never would. It didn't seem right to just go out on the internet and download some how-to video.

That flinch, though, had been real. I needed to get home as soon as possible to keep on schedule. Loading my bounty into the van we used for the inn, I lowered my head and closed my eyes as the EMTs slowly wheeled Emma out on a gurney.

There was no need to rush her and the proceedings, since there was no way to save her at this point. Somehow, that image seemed sadder than seeing her pressed against the glass and not breathing.

As I closed the back doors on the van, I heard a commotion behind me and turned to see Taboo lunging at the end of his leash toward the ambulance, where they were also closing the back doors. I paused and squeezed my eyes shut. Yes, I was going to do this thing that I really shouldn't do, but I didn't feel like I had a choice.

Approaching Norm, with my eyes wide open, I pulled him aside. "Would it be possible for me to take Taboo with me to the inn? I can keep him until Richard can pick him up. I know Wendy down at the animal shelter would probably take him, or maybe you have a pen at the station that he could stay in, but with what he just went through, it might be better for him to at least be with someone he knows."

Down the sidewalk, Taboo jerked so hard on the leash that he caught Phil off guard, and the man stumbled as the dog tried to get to his owner. The leash whipped out of his hand and flew along the sidewalk behind the dog as he raced ahead.

Without waiting for an answer from Norm—I'd apologize later—I dashed to meet Taboo in front of the ambulance doors. Grabbing the dog's collar, I put my other hand on the side of his face and then pressed my forehead to his.

"I know this is scary, baby boy. And I know you're sad, but we have to let them do their job. Why don't you come with me? You can have treats, and I bet Amelia would let you play with some of Daffy's toys. Maybe you could snuggle into one of the dog beds she has all over the cottage. How about that?"

Deep brown eyes looked into mine, and though I'd never actually seen a dog cry, I would have sworn he was. His jaw quivered, and his shoulders and ears drooped. I stroked his back and then hugged his neck. "It's going to be okay. We'll take care of you until Richard can come get you. It'll be okay. I promise." Or as okay as I could make it.

When I looked up, I caught Norm nodding at me and waving me off. "Go," he said, which I took to mean I could take the dog with me.

The van was only a few steps away, so it didn't take me long to get the passenger side front door open and coax the dog into jumping up and settling into the seat. He sat straight and didn't take his eyes off the ambulance as it drove off down the street.

While I circled the front of the van and slid into the driver's seat, I asked myself what I had just signed up for. I had a rehearsal to do and then dinner. I didn't need a new dog in the house, no matter how short a time it took Richard to get here. But I also had a soft spot for animals, and I just couldn't have left Taboo there to fend for himself or go to a shelter. No matter how much I trusted Wendy to do her best job, she also had a lot going on with a recent case of a hoarder's house with about fifty dogs in the backyard being raided. She was still trying to find homes for all those animals, and adding a dog who was going through grief to the mix would not be good for anyone.

The drive was short back to the inn, thankfully, but Taboo hardly even moved once he circled the front seat and lay down with his head tucked under one of his paws.

I had no idea what I was going to do when we got back and parked, but I'd figure it out. I was quick like that.

Pulling around to the spot in front of the garage, I turned the van off and looked over at Taboo. "So, here's what we're going to do. We're going to get you out and then see who you take to the most. I know this is scary, and you're sad, but I promise that things are going to get better just as soon as Richard gets here. It won't be what it was before, and you're still going to be sad, but it will be better."

Taboo lifted his head for just a moment and then froze in place, but a second later, it was like the fight went out of him, and he sank back down onto the seat.

Dean waved to me from the yard, completely unaware of what I had gotten us into. I waved back just as Taboo popped up in the front seat. Dean's smile fell into a frown, and then he rolled his eyes. Fair enough, but he'd understand once I had a chance to tell him that this time I wasn't going to be involved.

"What's up?" he said, approaching slowly as I exited the driver's seat and closed the van door behind me.

"Emma passed, and I found her at the shop. It's not murder, so don't worry. But Taboo was not leaving, and I was afraid to send him to the shelter right now. He'll only be here until Richard can pick him up."

"I'm so sorry to hear that. However long is fine. I'm sure we'll figure something out."

We both glanced over at the dog. Taboo stayed on guard in the front seat, but he was no longer paying attention to us. He was looking out at something to the right. I followed his gaze instead of answering Dean and smiled when I saw who was approaching. Poobah, who had gone into the flower shop weekly when his Grand Duchess, as we called my grandmother, had been alive. She'd passed six years ago. But he still went in weekly to chat with Emma and Richard and to pet Taboo, who had been a tiny puppy when he'd first started going in a decade ago, when Emma had opened her store.

I opened the door and leaned in. "You want to go see Poobah, don't you? He's right there, if you want to see him." Instead of coming to my side, Taboo pressed his nose to the window.

Maybe he didn't like to cross over the captain's chairs?

"Do we have a visitor?" Poobah asked, picking up his pace while also keeping his eyes on me.

"We have a very sad situation. Emma passed over, and Taboo was in the shop at the time. Rick's stuck at the campground, so I agreed to bring the dog home with me until things get sorted out."

"I felt a shift in things about forty minutes ago and was talking to Earl at the time. He saw a spirit pass, but didn't know who it was."

"Was she peaceful?" I really wanted her to have gone peacefully.

"As far as I know. But this little guy is going to struggle." Poobah placed his hand against the passenger side window. Taboo lifted his paw to the window and cried.

"We can let him out. He still has a leash on if you can grab it," I said, reaching for the handle.

"He won't need that." Poobah kept eye contact with the dog as he pulled up on the handle with one hand and then reached out to touch the quivering dog with his other.

Taboo settled right down and put his nose into Poobah's hand. Glancing over at me, my grandfather shook his head. "Will you need me at rehearsal, dear? I don't have a part really other than watching you start the rest of your life in happiness, and that's for tomorrow."

"No, we're good, but you might want to stop in for dinner."

"Oh, I won't want to miss that, especially since I heard Glennis has pulled out all the stops for this one."

"I heard the same thing." The dog and man had not taken their eyes off each other for even a second. What was going on there? "Do you want me to grab some of Daffy's food for you?"

"No, we're fine. I am going to be using the laundry room for the next hour or so, if you could please tell everyone to stay out for now." He nodded as if he and Taboo had come to an agreement.

Strange, but not that strange. Dogs understood much more than we gave them credit for, sometimes.

"Okay," I said, putting a hand on Taboo's head as he let himself out of the car, trailing the leash behind him. He sat like a good boy right in front of Poobah with his tongue lolled out, the leash draped behind him, still on the seat of the van.

I snapped it off his collar and handed it to Poobah, and then the two headed off toward the house, walking side by side as if tethered to each other with some invisible rope.

"Is it just me, or was that strange?" I asked Dean when he put his arm around my waist, then drew me back so he could rest his chin on my head. It was one of my favorite places to be.

"I'm not sure about strange, maybe just different. If we labeled everything in this family that was outside the norm as strange, there wouldn't be a single thing that wasn't strange in this family, which would then become the norm."

"That makes sense to me, even with your convoluted ways, and I love you for that." I smiled as he laughed above me.

"Thank you, I think."

"You're welcome, I'm sure." I gave his hands at my waist a squeeze. "Now we need to go do the rehearsal. I'll explain to everyone why Poobah isn't with us for the event, and let them know that Emma is gone, but was being taken care of. Then we can get to whatever Glennis made for dinner. Oh, and her seating chart should delight almost everyone."

"Almost?"

I snickered. "Yeah, you'll see."

And I left it there as I watched Poobah lead a very solemn Taboo into the house. The dog leaned into Poobah, and I understood, thinking that the older man had all the answers in the world. Fortunately, right now, I don't have too many questions because all the answers seemed to be holding me in a place that I didn't want to ever leave.

After tomorrow, things would be in the bag, and I could rest. Of course, I probably had just jinxed myself, but apparently, I was willing to take that chance. I didn't even reach up to knock on the wooden arch above us.

Chapter 3

If I had jinxed myself, it didn't come to bite me at the rehearsal at all. Even Moose walked down the aisle without a single issue. And if the way Dean looked at me as I exited the double French doors out of the dining room was any indication, I was going to be crying in gratitude before I even made it halfway down the aisle on my father's arm.

How did I get so lucky? I wasn't sure, and I didn't want to question it too much, because sometimes things just happened that were supposed to. It wasn't my job to question them, but just to appreciate them. I didn't have to tear them apart to find out how they worked and why.

With Sharon watching from the sidelines, we went through the words we were supposed to say and where we were supposed to stand. And it all went like clockwork. I finally let out a breath of relief when it was time to go back into the dining room for dinner.

After saying goodbye to Sharon and thanking her for all her hard work, Dean and I stood in the gazebo by ourselves for a minute. Dean circled my wrist with his big hand and gently tugged to keep me in place while everyone else kept walking and chatting amongst themselves.

"You ready for this?" he asked, bracketing my other wrist and drawing me in slowly so that he could move his arms around my waist. I nestled against him, front to front. "Because tomorrow's the day you say the words, and then you're stuck with me forever."

I giggled, but then took in the seriousness of his expression. Reaching up, I cradled his cheek. "I have never in my life been more ready for something. I never even dreamed I could be with someone who was so imperfectly perfect. And if I had the dream, I wouldn't have been able to encompass all the wonderful things you are."

He settled his cheek into my palm and then turned to kiss the center, right where my lifelines crossed. "We'll fight," he said.

"We already have and made it through."

"You might not like actually living with me full time. Right now, you can still kick me out if I'm taking up too much of your space, but after tomorrow, I'm not leaving for anything."

"You wouldn't be able to leave anyway because I'd put a magic barrier on the doors, and you wouldn't get through, no matter how much you wanted to."

He laughed, and I felt the reverberation in my chest. "You wouldn't."

"Oh, I most certainly would, so I wouldn't start testing me on that as your first act of husbandly irritation."

"I love you, Roxy."

"Then I'm lucky I love you back, Dean."

He tipped my head up by my chin and leaned down to place the softest and yet most sensual kiss on my lips that I'd ever experienced. I was fast-moving past the stunned feeling into the never want to leave feeling when Mena yelled out the door. "I am not going to follow your freaking seating chart, Roxy! Get in here and change it before I set it on fire!"

"The siren calls," I said, snickering.

"Are you going to answer?"

"Of course not."

"Who's she sitting next to?" He tucked my short hair back behind my ear and left his index finger there for just a moment as he looked deep into my eyes. I hoped he would always love everything he saw in there.

"Micah."

He gasped and laughed at the same time. "He's not even in the wedding party."

"Well, Glennis had thoughts about that, and then overrode any hesitation to make him be part of things simply because she could. I heard he grudgingly said yes when she told him he was going to be here taking action shots during the rehearsal dinner and then tomorrow. And for his trouble, she would make him those potstickers he can't get enough of."

"Not a bad bargain."

"But one that could go off the rails if Mena tries to convince him that he doesn't want to be here, or that he would really like to eat his dinner out in the foyer."

"We should get in there then..." he said, but then kissed me again, and another minute or so was taken up by this lovely man who was everything.

A gong went off in the house, and I full-out laughed against his lips. "Things are about to get real if Glennis is banging the dinner gong. We really have to go."

"Fine, fine, fine." He hooked an arm over my shoulders, and I settled into where I would like to always be. But there was a small hint of sadness that Rick would never again get to drape an arm over Emma's shoulders. I tried not to let the thought put a pall on the moment. There was nothing I could do about it, but I did hope whatever had happened to Emma wasn't painful, and she was on the next plane, living her best afterlife.

The dining room was hopping when we walked in, but as soon as everyone saw us, a huge cheer went up from around the table. Even Mena, who was smack up against Micah at the far end of the dining table, stopped her scowling long enough to throw out a "woohoo," and then she went back to scowling. I had a feeling in my gut that she had probably tried every which way to get away from being stuck next to the man she had been flirting with over the past several months. Well, they had been flirting until something happened between them, and she'd shut herself off from walking around town with him and seeing him every chance she could get.

I hadn't been able to get her to tell me what had happened, but that same gut told me it was something that could be worked out if she'd unbend a little.

I wasn't too worried about it now. It could wait another day, as long as she behaved herself in the interim.

And there were so many other faces to take in and enjoy that they were here to celebrate our big day. My oldest sister, Anjanetta, had a huge smile on her face as she sat next to her husband, Clive. Both had been dragooned into the wedding as a bridesmaid and a groomsman, respectively. I hadn't expected Dean to want Clive to be at his side at the altar, but Dean had said it rounded out his numbers and that he wanted my family to be his family, too.

They were seated next to Mena and Micah, and then there were my parents, Diana and Belmont. They were often out on the road, doing their traveling thing for most of the year, so we rarely were all under the same roof at the same time. But here we were, and that filled my heart with a whole lot of happiness.

Dean's area of the table was much smaller with just his brother, Caper, nephew, Isaac, and niece, Amelia. But there were no divisions here, and everyone went back to talking loudly across and around the table after the short celebration. As one does when the room is filled with people who have something to say.

Glennis came out of the kitchen, followed by the two women who helped her in the kitchen, Clara and Taylor. They loaded up the sideboard with steaming dishes of potstickers and breaded chicken, sauces galore, steak on shish kabobs, and a whole lot of pasta, from fettuccine to thin spaghetti, along with those tortellini I loved, and an array of corkscrew noodles.

At first, I thought, how on Earth were we going to eat all of this, and then looked out across the room and realized it would all be gone well before it even cooled a little, and I was good with that.

Dean and I took our seats at the head of the table next to a smiling Poobah.

"How's Taboo doing?" I asked as I reached for my glass of water. The line had already started forming, and I probably should have jumped right in to make sure I got what I wanted from Glennis's generous spread. However, I had her three hundred sixty-five days of the year, and if I didn't get it tonight, it didn't mean I couldn't have it any other day of the week.

"Taboo's settling into your old rooms. I had planned on using the laundry room, but there wasn't anywhere comfortable for him. He seemed happy to curl up on the couch in the sitting room, though, and only whined a few times when I left. I stood outside the door and listened to make sure it didn't go on for too long."

My old rooms were sparsely furnished, since Dean and I had taken over the third floor of the inn. We'd made some significant changes up there, while also giving ourselves a bunch more square footage than I'd had in my bedroom and sitting room on the first floor. When Poobah and the Grand Duchess had run the inn, they'd actually lived off-site, but I wasn't ready to do that just yet, and Dean had been ecstatic to move to the top floor.

"Any word from Rick?" I grabbed a roll out of the basket in front of me and buttered it as if my life depended on it. Well, maybe not my life, but definitely my happiness, if these were the rolls Glennis only made for special occasions.

And I knew they were with the first bite. Oh, my yum! Someone was going to have to move the basket, or I'd devour every one of them and possibly stab someone with a fork if they tried to take one. Dean knew me well enough not to even have to be asked. He did, however, leave three on my small bread plate before he passed the rolls down the other side of the table.

Poobah snickered, but then sobered right up. "I did some scrying, and I'm afraid things are not quite as they seemed. Taboo might have calmed down, but there's a frequency in him that is far higher than it should be, and I'm not sure what it means."

Well, that didn't sound awesome in the least. "Is it..." I gulped, the bread lodging in my throat. I swallowed and tried again. "Is it something that will need to be handled right now?" I looked out across the table. We couldn't do anything with magic due to how many people were in the room who knew nothing about the extra powers we had. But if I had to leave, then I would do so in order to protect anyone and everyone in this room.

Poobah placed his hand over mine. "It's nothing concrete at the moment, and you don't have to save the whole world. I'm fine with keeping the dog happy until things get sorted out. He's no trouble at all. In fact, it's nice to have another being in the vicinity. I'd forgotten how many things I used to run by Gozar when she was around."

Gozar had been the yorkie he'd had with my grandmother, the dog who had stood at the door every day for a week, waiting for her human to return from the hairstylist. But she never came home because she had passed away.

"Maybe we could look into the shelter for a companion." Dean leaned forward to be able to look past me at Poobah.

"We'll see." Poobah smiled and patted Dean's shoulder behind my back. "Let's get through this whole thing first, and then life can go back to what it was. I'll keep it in mind, though."

Everyone settled down once they were stuffing their mouths with the delicious food Glennis and her staff had prepared. I was so happy to see my wonderful cook happier than she had been in years. And it had been worth all the angst last time we'd had a murderer in the area for her to be able to get out of her own head and embrace the life she'd created instead of the one she'd always dreamed of. She was still as sassy as all get out, but now it was tempered with far more humor and a lot less meanness. I was here for it.

I snagged her as she headed back to the kitchen with her hands empty. "I thought you were going to put out places for all of you to join us. Are you eating in the kitchen, instead?"

Glennis nodded. "The three of us talked, and we still have a lot to organize for tomorrow, so we're going to eat, drink, and be merry, while also strategically fabulous for tomorrow. For that, we need to be at our battle stations. You understand."

"Of course, but if you want to come out for dessert, then please do."

"Oh, I made something special just for us. We don't need your desserts." She chuckled, a little villainy to my ears, but I let it pass.

Finally, the line had died down enough for me to feel like it was time to go fill my plate to heaping. Dean followed along behind me closely, and we each took some very large helpings, since it was a given that he'd probably eat off my plate, and I'd definitely eat off of his.

Mena tapped her glass with a spoon, drawing everyone's attention to her. "I'd like to propose a toast," she said, raising her glass of sparkling apple cider and standing. "To the man who seems to get away with everything, no matter how bad it might be." She was glancing around the table, not landing on any one male in particular. What was she doing? "I want to let you know that I admire you, full stop. Although after the full stop, I also want to say that I find you fascinating, full stop, and frustrating. Another full stop. A little irritating, too." She tapped a finger to her lips and cocked her head to the side, staring at the ceiling.

Our mom tried to pull her back down into her seat, but Mena was having none of it. Was she drunk? When did she manage that? And why did she have to do it tonight?

"For those who are wondering if I'm intoxicated, the answer is no, but I do think I might have been drugged."

And then, she fell over backward, right into Micah's waiting arms.

Chapter 4

Everyone at the table jumped up at once and ran for Mena. She was in good hands and didn't need anyone but Micah fanning her face and speaking softly to her. Her eyelids fluttered, and the smile grew on her face when she found herself being looked over by the man she had flirted with endlessly, until something happened, and it all dried up.

That lasted for about five seconds before she scrambled away from his embrace and patted her hair. "I'm fine, I'm fine. I don't know what happened there, but I feel better now."

"You're sure?" I asked.

"I'm positive. It was like something came over me, but then my system shut it down. Whatever 'it' is."

"You're going to want to get checked out."

"Maybe," she said, still patting her hair. To see if it was still there, or to tamp it down? I wasn't sure, but at least she looked better and more like herself. The spectacle of her being uncomfortable and stuck with Micah was a sight to see, and I was here for it, now that I could tell she was all right.

With the slight pivot back toward normal, we had issues that we couldn't ignore, and I had questions about her previously being certain she was drugged.

Everyone stepped back as I waded into the middle of the crowd. "Mena, I need you to think for a second. Did you drink or eat anything that could have hurt you?"

I glanced at her place setting, knowing there was no way that anyone in this house would have poisoned her. And if it was poison, then how did no one else who had partaken of this huge buffet have the same effects?

But then my eye was caught by a box of chocolates. Mena still hadn't answered me, and she'd started rocking back and forth, swaying as she smiled and hummed to herself. Maybe not poison, but something wasn't right.

I grabbed her chin and forced her face around to look directly at me. "Mena, did you eat the chocolates?"

"Hmm, uh-huh, all the chocolates were good, one tasted just a little bit bitter, but since I was bitter, maybe that was just my fault." She sighed a big sigh, and then started humming again.

Holding her face in my hand to keep her still, I glanced around the room. "Did anyone else eat the chocolates?"

When I got back a chorus of no's, I found my mom in the crowd and locked gazes with her. She nodded, which made me feel better. "Okay, you're going to be fine."

"I will be, now that Micah is holding my hand." She said the words with a dreamy cast to them and a soft smile on her face.

"I'm going to have to ask Micah to go into the kitchen and get some ice," our mom said, brooking no argument. Mena might be the one to be able to manipulate people. It was her power, but Mom was a whole other creature when it came to people obeying her.

"There's ice right…" Dean started, but then trailed off when I shot him a look.

"Micah, if you wouldn't mind?" Mom asked, taking Mena's hand from him.

My youngest sister mewled, but Micah stood up quickly and immediately headed over to the door into the kitchen. As soon as the door closed behind him, Mom leaned over Mena and rested her fingertips on her daughter's temple. From an outsider, it would probably look like she was simply checking for any kind of fever. We needed the illusion. The cook and helpers could see things on the television camera in the kitchen, and we had to keep this between those who had, or knew about, talents. In reality, Diana Gleason was murmuring under her breath, clearing things out of Mena's system with words and energy instead of sending her to the hospital to get her stomach pumped.

"I'm back," Micah said as he sailed into the room. He handed over the cup of ice, then immediately took Mena's hand again. In his other hand was his phone. "I should call the EMTs. If she's been poisoned, then we need to have someone check her out and get rid of whatever was in that chocolate."

"She's going to be okay, Micah," Mom said in a soothing voice that spoke volumes, even if you weren't listening. "She does have a slight allergy to certain kinds of chocolate. That bitter one was the kind she's not supposed to eat, and she must not have checked the packaging before popping it into her mouth. It's just a quick thing, so there's no need for intervention. I promise. I'm her mom, and if I thought she needed to be seen by a doctor, I'd already be driving her there. We just need to get her to bed, and then she'll be fine in about an hour. Let's give her the opportunity to heal in surroundings she knows."

Micah was transfixed by every word Diana said. But he also looked like he was fighting with himself, his brain trying to balk against the difference between what he was being told and what he felt he had seen and knew.

In the end, though, he set his phone down on the table and covered Mena's hand with both of his. I breathed out a sigh of relief as I nodded at him and slowly coaxed Mena out of her chair by grabbing her forearms and pulling her toward me. Micah was having none of that, though, and simply scooped her up in his arms, then hauled her out to the lobby. Although, to be fair, haul might not have been the right word, since it was too brash. He cradled her in his arms, and when she started crying, he touched his forehead to hers and murmured something to her. Within seconds, she quieted down, and he stood in the lobby waiting for someone to lead him to where she slept. Interesting that he didn't know...

Mom walked out of the dining room with a commanding stride and beckoned Micah to follow her. He had already been in motion, though, with my sister firmly in his hold. Since Mena was in capable hands, I went back to the dining room and used a cloth napkin from the breadbasket to pick up the box of chocolates and moved it to the front desk. "Don't anyone touch this, okay?"

I even took a second to grab a sticky note from one of the cubbies under the counter and used a Sharpie to put *Do Not Touch* on the box.

Dean joined me at the desk and put his hand over mine. "She's going to be fine, right?"

"Yes. Yes, of course, yeah. I'm sure Mom has it under control, but I'm very concerned about the chocolates. Is Mena really allergic to a specific type of chocolate, or was my mom just moving things along? I don't remember my sister ever being allergic to anything, but Mom could have told that story to reassure Micah. I don't like this, no matter which way it goes."

"Do you think we should call Norm to see if he can test for a poison?"

My breath froze in my throat as I bit my lip. No need to panic. None. *Zero.* "I think we should wait until I can talk to my mom about what she really thinks happened. If it was something Mena is allergic to, and I just didn't know about it, I don't want to bring the police in. These chocolates came from the flower shop as a gift to me, and Emma is dead. If Norm thinks the two are related, and Mena was poisoned, then we make everything blow up in a possible murder thing, instead of waiting and making sure that it wasn't just body chemistry issues."

"If you think that's best, then that's what we'll go with."

I released a slow breath and nodded at Dean. "Thank you. I appreciate it. I'm hoping we're doing the right thing at this point, but I'm not sure. I don't want to be an alarmist, though."

"I get that. You don't have to explain yourself. I'm on your side."

"And I appreciate that." But I still bit my lip while hoping I was doing the right thing.

It wasn't until my mom finally came out of the room, where they'd taken Mena, towing Micah behind her, that I was finally able to breathe again and stop gnawing on my lip, which was nearly raw now.

"You shouldn't do that right before your wedding, my dear." Mom swiped a finger over my stinging bottom lip, and the pain immediately went away. Such was the power of Diana.

"How is M—"

"Let me get Micah on his way, dear. He has important things to do. I'll talk to you in just a moment." She smiled at the man and then kissed him on the cheek at the front door. "Please let me know when you've found the information we were talking about. I so appreciate this, Micah. You're a doll."

He looked a little bewildered as he left, pulling the door closed behind him, but that could happen with my mom sometimes. She had several different talents, at low levels for the most part. Her compulsion to get people not to question her, though, was second to none.

"Okay, he's gone, now tell me what happened." I crossed my arms over my chest to hold my anxiety in check.

"We should take this somewhere more private," she said, looking around as if a bunch of people were about to cascade out of some hidden door and shine a klieg light on her.

"Just tell me if she was poisoned, allergic to something in the chocolate, or drunk."

Diana shook her head. "Drunk would have been much easier. Even allergies would have been less hectic than what was going on in her system. It wasn't just a poison. It had hints of a spell, and a few chaotic charms that I haven't heard in decades."

Oh, I did not like that at all. "Like what?"

"I don't actually know the core spell that was going on, but it triggered something in my mind that I haven't thought of in years. I know you're not going to like this, but I need to talk to your father and Poobah before I say anything more on that."

She was right, I didn't like that at all either. "Should we be on guard? Is something bad going to happen to us all?"

Cupping my cheek, she kissed my forehead. "Roxy, always so tuned in to saving everyone else, always so worried. Sweetheart, I promise I will let you know if there is something more going on. In fact, I'd already have a thousand wards up on this establishment, I promise. You do come by that worry honestly. I've always admitted that. I promise it's just a few things I want to ask the men who've been around longer than me before I go any further."

Dean laced his fingers through mine and raised my hand to his lips. "Okay?"

It could have been a question of whether I was okay or if I was okay with this. Either way, I nodded.

"Please let me know as soon as possible."

"Of course, I will," Mom said. "You can come with me if you want, but it might be easier with fewer hands in this particular pot until we have it stirred correctly."

I fought against the need to be involved at every level. Normally, I was used to being the one leading things, not letting others handle it, and then getting back to me. Although that wasn't entirely true, and I knew it. I had many people who helped out in this establishment and didn't feel the need to bring me every little thing. I'd just been reminded of that recently, and I needed to trust that those around me had all our best interests in mind, and if they needed something, they'd bring it to me. In any other case, they were more than capable of handling what I couldn't and letting me know after it was done.

Mom started walking away, as if the conversation was done, and she'd get back to me when she had more information.

"One last question, though, and then I'll let you go," I said.

"What?" she asked as she turned around.

"Do I need to call Norm in on this? Was Emma's death a murder?"

She cocked her head to the side and looked up at the ceiling. "I'm not sure, to be honest. I wasn't there, so I don't know what the energy in the store was like. I don't want to say yes at this point because I don't want to cause concern if there is none. Can you give me an hour? I will get back to you as soon as I can. In fact, I could get back to you sooner if you'd let me go do what I need to do."

She smiled to soften what she was saying, but I still bit my lip.

"What did I tell you about that? I can only heal so much on the same spot, darling. Careful."

I unclenched my teeth from my poor bottom lip and nodded. "You know where to find me."

"Of course I do, and I promise to come back to you as soon as I have some more clarity on what is happening. In the meantime, why don't you go check on Mena and assure her that she didn't say anything that she shouldn't have while in her stupor and fawning over Micah?"

"You want me to lie to her?"

"Absolutely. And take Dean with you. He can boost the lie and make sure it sticks." She winked at my fiancé, and I wasn't sure why.

But he smiled, and then she was gone into the billiard room, and I was left to hope for the best.

"What did she mean by that wink?" Dean asked, still holding my hand in his.

"I have no idea and was wondering the same thing myself." Could it be that she thought he had a talent, a latent one? We'd all thought that the talent had come through Amelia's mom, Caper's significant other, who was currently serving her sentence in jail, but maybe there was more to that story than we had thought.

I needed time to consider that, and maybe come up with a way to test Dean out, but that was going to have to wait. Mena stuck her head over the staircase on the second floor and shouted for me to bring her an ice cream. With sprinkles. And whipped cream. And a cherry on top.

"I guess I'd better go handle that," I said. "Do you think I could send Aunt Hellen in first?"

Dean laughed and also kissed me on the forehead. "Glennis will be happy to make her a sundae instead of letting her in there herself. At least this way the dishes won't end up left in the sink overnight."

"There is a lot of truth in that, Dean Winchester." Before we went anywhere, I turned into his arms, lay my head on his chest, and just breathed in—the scent of him, his calm, his strength. I closed my eyes for just a second when he ran his hand over my back and placed his chin on the top of my head.

"It's all going to be okay. I promise that. No matter what is going on, it will be okay. I won't have it any other way." I could feel his jaw moving on my crown.

"But what if..."

"Nope, we're not doing that right now. Right now, we're going to get Mena her ice cream so she can calm herself down, and then we're going to wait to hear from your mom. Then we're going to get married tomorrow."

"I love you," I said against his chest.

"And fortunately for both of us, I love you, too. Now, let's get cracking with the whipped cream can. You know how much she loves that stuff. Almost as much as I love you."

That got me to laugh finally. Things weren't perfect and I was still very concerned they might never be again, but at least in this moment, things were going to be okay. I had to believe that.

Chapter 5

Once we got Mena set up and ready with all the ice cream ridiculousness she could ever hope for, plus an extra swirl of whipped cream, Dean and I went into the library to wait for word from my mother. I'd passed the billiards room twice in my pursuit of Mena's happiness, and there was a definite murmur of intense conversation in there, but no distinguishable words.

"What is taking them so freaking long?" I asked, very aware that only thirty-five minutes of my mom's requested hour had passed. Yes, I was impatient. I'd made peace with that years ago, and other people needed to also.

"You could take a look in a book," Dean said, perched on the edge of one of the fluffy armchairs scattered around the vast two-story library.

"I'd probably do better trying to ride that rolling ladder from one end of the track to the other."

"You never did tell me the whole story of that adventure."

I burst out laughing. "Adventure. Yeah, that's a good word for it, and I will forever keep it to myself." I sighed. "I just wish I knew what was going on."

"You could have gone with your mom and talked with your dad and Poobah. She did invite you."

"You have to know my mother really well in order to see that she very much did not want me there because I'd just be another cog in a gummed-up machine."

"But you trust her to get you answers, so why not see if the books have anything to offer up when she comes in. I'm hearing a humming off to the left if you want to go on a little adventure, not the swinging from the ladder kind."

I shot him a squinty-eyed look to gauge if he was trying to distract me. However, in my peripheral vision, I saw a sparkle, more like a glow, coming from a section of the library I rarely, if ever, went to. The section Poobah absolutely could not do without. Repair manuals for vintage cars. There was room for all kinds of books here, and I had never asked him to take it out, but it didn't really fit the aesthetic of the rest of the offerings. And yet, if one of those books wanted to talk to me, who was I to say no?

As I started walking over and around the corner of a study table I'd salvaged from the basement, I was pleased to see Dean join me. The closer I got, the more intense the glow got, until I was almost blinded by the time I got my hands on the book. And as soon as I slid it out of its spot on the shelf, I promptly dropped it because it was hot. Not scorching, but definitely unnatural in the sheer heat of the cover. Looking around, I made sure it wasn't in the direct line of the sun or under any kind of heat lamp. So, what was up with that?

And, when it landed on the floor, it fell open to a page that had no pictures of how to fix your catalytic converter or what to do with a busted tail pipe. It did, however, have a note stashed in between the pages.

I was almost afraid to touch it in case it started scorching my fingertips, but then there was Dean with a ballpoint pen and one of the armchair doilies my Great Aunt Agnes had made whenever she vacationed here.

"Just use the pen to move it off the book and then the crochet thing to pick it up." He handed them over to me.

"Got it." I did just as he said, hoping against all other hope that once the paper fell to the floor, it would not light the whole place on fire. I'd already seen the police and EMTs today, so I did not want to add the fire department just so I could claim a trifecta of problem child tendencies.

Miraculously, it did not burn the carpet, and, as soon as it was off the page of the repair book, everything cooled down immediately. Bizarre, and something I would have to run past my mother when we talked. She was experiencing things she had not in years, and I was experiencing things I had never heard of. That was a little scarier, at least until I found out what she had been dealing with. Eek, so many tabs open in my brain and not enough bandwidth to keep them all up.

I could do this, though. One step, one thing, at a time.

Using the doily edge, I picked up just the corner of the ragged edge of the piece of paper and then just stood there. Where should I put this? Honestly, I wanted to throw it down on the ground and just wait for someone else to help. And yet, more than that, I wanted to know what I was dealing with before I brought other hands on deck for this new discovery.

"Thoughts?" I asked, looking up at Dean to see if he had any insight into the note.

"You're asking me? I'm totally new to this whole thing, Roxy. I'm not going to be any help."

"And yet, it's often the people who are new to this kind of thing who have the best questions because they have no assumptions and no long-held beliefs." I dropped the note onto a study table and then moved it from the original spot after a second with the end of the pen to see if there was a scorch mark at all. Nothing. That was good. And even better when I couldn't feel any heat radiating from the paper or the surface underneath it.

We were in business! Well, I was hoping that was true, anyway.

With that in mind, I was cautious when I flipped the paper over. I had no idea what to expect, and that made my touch very jittery when I grabbed the edge of the small, aging square of yellowing paper.

"Beware the lies you tell, and those that are told to you. Silence is not the key. It is the lock." I read it out loud the first time, but then read it three more times to myself in my head before looking up at Dean. "Do you have any idea what this means?"

When he shook his head, I shifted it so that he could read it from where he was standing. He didn't touch it, just stared at it with his hand on his chin. He cocked his head left, and then right, then moved in a little closer to squint at the words. "Does it look to you like there's something more under the writing, like impressions that would have been made by someone digging a pen in that had no ink?"

He stepped back from the table as I rounded the corner. Leaning forward with my hands clasped behind my back, I tried to decipher what he was talking about. Was it similar to the impressions Poobah had talked about that he'd been able to see on the green matting on the pool table? He'd been so adamant that whole battle plans had been written into the table, and they'd left impressions not necessarily discernible by the naked eye. But when he'd put tracing paper over the mat and then used a pencil to shade the paper, the words had popped out as if being written for the first time.

"We need to run this by Poobah." I gingerly took the paper between my thumb and pointer finger with the doily protecting us both.

"Do you want me to go get him?" Dean asked.

"No, this has to be taken to the source, and since I haven't seen my mother yet, I'm going to assume they're all still in the billiards room. If you'll get the doors, I'll carry this thing like it's the most fragile of China."

And I did just that as we exited the library, then turned left to head back to the room where I hoped to find my grandfather, mother, and father. I didn't want to interrupt them with anything while they were discussing old charms and curses, but this was important.

Dean was quick to open the library door and then the billiard room door, two steps in front of me, like I was carrying a bomb that needed to be disposed of, instead of a piece of dead tree.

In my peripheral vision, I saw my dad leaning hard on the edge of the pool table while my mother removed darts from the board on the far wall. Poobah sat on a high stool, chalking a pool stick with a serious frown on his aging face.

They had all been talking at once, quite vehemently, when Dean had opened the door. But that all stopped at the same moment, like someone had hit pause on a television.

It didn't stop me from moving forward, though, and putting down my burden onto the marble counter where Poobah kept a decanter or two of liquor, if you knew where to look.

As soon as I set it down, the letters glowed in a way they had not before. They glimmered and then rose from the paper, swirling in a cloud of dark gold sparkles, but not forming into any words as they previously had. I had never seen anything like it before, and I was so entranced that I didn't realize I had raised my hand to touch them until my mother was by my side, clasping her fingers around mine.

"Let's be careful with this one, sweetheart. I'm not sure I like the feeling I'm getting off of it, and it can wait for a moment while we cleanse a few things. Sound good?"

Not really, part of my brain said, and I could feel my whole body being drawn forward, twisting to find a way around her. But the other part of my brain was operating in survival mode, demanding that I not, under any circumstances, touch those glitters. There was something wrong with them. But why only now? Who in the room was the person who had activated them to perform differently than when it was just me and Dean in the library? Why now? What had changed?

I wanted the answers to all those questions, but I also wanted to keep my sanity.

So, I shut my eyes and took a pause of my own to unlock whatever was trying to desperately chain my body into a response that went against everything I believed in.

For fifteen seconds, I counted things I could smell, things I could touch, things I could hear, and things I could taste.

I only got that far when I opened my eyes again, and the sparkles were still there in the air, but I no longer had to touch them. That disconnect held as I took a better look at the sparkles themselves and saw that some of them were the gold I had come to expect, but the others were a dirty brown, mixing with the gold to make everything look like shiny mud.

"What is happening here? It looks like something is making the normal sparkles look dirty." I no longer wanted to touch them, but that didn't mean I didn't want to understand them. Especially since they weren't coalescing into any kind of letters, but instead were just hanging in the air, their movement getting slower and slower until finally they came to a standstill.

At that point, Poobah rose from his perch on the high stool and approached the sparkles. They didn't move at all, just hung there like a small portrait of chaos.

My mom and dad joined him, and still they didn't move.

But then Dean took one step forward, and they burst into a frenzy that I could not keep track of. Why hadn't they done that when it was just the two of us in the library? Why here? Why now?

The piece of paper trembled on the marble bar, as if convulsing.

What was happening here?

"Dean was the one who said there were indentations on the paper, as if it had been written on with an invisible pen or marked before the actual message on the paper was written. And Poobah, you've said before that there were a ton of words written on top of the pool table that you were able to take rubbings of." I didn't ask for permission. I simply grabbed the paper from the marble and used the doily to toss it onto the pool table to my right.

The trembling paper lay still for about ten seconds, nothing happening for what seemed like an eternity as we all watched. And then it started bunching and stretching, bunching and stretching, as it moved itself across the table, like a planchette on a Ouija board. I'd never seen anything like it, and it was both fascinating and horrifying at the same time.

Had something been unleashed in the house that we weren't prepared to deal with? There was a reason, a very good one, that no one was allowed to bring one of those boards into the house. They could open doors to things and beings who were not of this world, and we were very much against that here at The Charmed Inn.

The paper finally landed in a spot directly at the curve in the right corner pocket of the table. One edge of it flipped up, as if waving, and then the small square burst into flames.

Chapter 6

Every room in the house had a fire extinguisher, per the building code. But for the life of me, I could not remember where it was, or what I was supposed to do with it, while I watched that flame dance on the green matting of the pool table. I was not alone in being stunned as my mom, dad, and Poobah didn't move either. But Dean, ever the hero, darted his hand under the cue rack and came up ready for battle.

However, the paper flamed out in the next second, and to all of our surprise, there was nothing left of the paper. There were no ashes. It hadn't even left a single scorch mark on the green beneath it. It was as if the thing had never existed, even though I knew, without a shadow of a doubt, that it had in fact been right there just a moment ago.

Fortunately, Dean stopped himself from unleashing the foam onto the table, where there was no longer a danger of the fire spreading. There was no fire at all. And now nothing to clean up.

"Well, that's bizarre," Mom said, speaking for all of us, as far as I was concerned.

Everyone started talking at the same time. Everyone except Poobah, who walked back to that marble counter and pulled a key from his pocket to unlock the cabinet under the table.

He retrieved the notebooks he'd used to take impressions of the things that had been written on the pool table over the centuries and started flipping pages with a precision that would have made a ticking clock or metronome proud.

I could hear him counting under his breath, even over the conversation going on with Dean and my parents, full of exclamations and questions. I went to stand next to my grandfather, but didn't interrupt him. I didn't want to throw off whatever rhythm he had going as he looked through a gigantic bound notebook with hundreds of pages of rubbings.

He flipped one more page, then flipped back to the last page and rested his palm on the gray and white. "This one. Rise and shine, show yourself in this time."

Everything stopped in the room, as it had earlier, but this was different. The people behind us literally froze in place, cut off in mid-sentence and mid-breath. There was a stasis happening, and I briefly wondered if it was also happening throughout the rest of the house or just this particular room. I also wondered how I had made it through and was still able to talk and breathe.

"What are you doing?" I finally whispered.

"Wait," Poobah said. "Just a moment more."

I did, and then took a step back in shock as the words on the page rose from the book in a cascade of sparkles. I'd looked at these books a hundred times since Poobah had shown them to me a year ago, and they'd never done anything like this.

"What..."

"Shh, let it do its thing without interruption. Five more seconds."

I counted those in my head and was rewarded when, right at the five-second mark, words formed in front of us.

"Beware of the chasm," I read out loud. I might have felt rewarded by the image of the words, but I was not happy with their potential meaning.

The sparkles turned black and fell back onto the book as they often did during my own explorations and questions with my talent. Did Poobah also have the gifts of bibliomancy? Why hadn't he taken me in hand and trained me instead of leaving me hanging when no one had really taken my gift seriously and had let me do more trial and error than learning?

It was going to have to be a question for a different time because the world came back up to speed, and my mom's phone started ringing.

"Micah, what did you find?" she asked with the speakerphone on.

"No poison, she died of a heart attack, the doctor and Rick both confirmed it. We also checked with her physician to see if it was something that could have happened so suddenly. He said he'd been warning her for months about the possibility due to her labs, and she would not take him seriously. So, no foul play, fortunately, I hope that helps and that you'll let Mena know..." He trailed off, but my mother smiled.

"I'll let her know. Thank you. You've just made my night, and I can't thank you enough. I'm sure Mena will be incredibly thankful and will show her gratitude tomorrow at the wedding."

His chuckle was a little nervous, and then he hung up with a quick goodbye.

After putting the phone down, she clapped her hands. Not to applaud anything, but to get everyone's attention. "No poison or murder, as you heard, and whatever you just did there, Dad, I do not like being paused so effectively without my permission. Don't do it again." She narrowed her eyes at him, but he just shrugged. "Everyone to bed. We have a big day tomorrow, and whatever chasm we're supposed to be aware of can be dealt with in our own time. I will not be forced to sacrifice a much-anticipated day because some magical bullshit is happening. It's waited this many centuries, it can wait a little longer."

And that was the final word on that, apparently.

***

An hour after we were all shepherded out of the billiard room and sent to our own rooms, I couldn't relax, and I was too hyped up to sleep yet. I was on the third floor, where Dean and I had been working to put together the place we would call home after we got married tomorrow.

We'd originally gone through the many different ways our home situation could work, from us moving to his apartment to us buying a house off the inn property, so he could have some space not attached to my job and career. I had lived in the rooms on the first floor for two years, and while they were fine for me, they did not fit the needs of more than one person living on their own. Dean had things that he, of course, wanted to bring with him, though really it was very little compared to my vast collection of books and candles, coasters and teacups.

But I had not wanted him to have to cram himself into the space that had been mine for those years and feel like it wasn't also his. Beyond that, I also hadn't been sure what to take down, so he could also have ownership of the space.

In the end, we'd put our heads together and eventually come up with taking over the top floor of the inn. Hardly anyone ever stayed up here, as I liked to keep the inn slightly under completely rented out at any time. And having the room downstairs to put in an office where I could work, then leave, instead of living in my workspace, would go a long way toward giving me the balance I now craved in this new phase of my life.

And tomorrow would begin our life here as Dean was going to move his things in after the wedding. Per him, he already had everything boxed up, but had wanted to wait until it was official to make the area his. Apparently, it would be like Christmas, in his eyes, getting to open everything and place it around the barely decorated room next to our bedroom. We'd put in a small galley kitchen, too, and had a sitting room, as well as a small dining nook. For the last two weeks, he had often been up here with me after the construction was done. But tonight, he had ideas on how things were supposed to work, so he had opted to stay with Caper in the small cottage at the back of the property so we wouldn't see each other before the wedding.

I won't lie, I fought hard against that rule, because it was just a superstition, but he was completely unmovable about it.

Which was why I hesitated to call him on the phone, even though he probably wasn't asleep yet either. I glanced out the upstairs window by moving the curtain aside and looked down at the small cottage. Maybe I should just text him. If he wasn't doing anything, he'd answer back. If not, it was just a small ding in the dark, not full-on ringing until I finally got shoved into voicemail.

I sent the text telling him I loved him and couldn't relax, that I was excited for tomorrow. And I left it there, even though I had a whole book I wanted to write about not feeling good about leaving things as we had left them. Beyond that, I also wanted to talk more about this chasm we were supposed to be aware of, and if I was being incredibly selfish by not telling Norm that things could be very wrong with the death of Emma.

Almost exactly a minute after I hit send, Dean responded that he was calling me. And five seconds later, I watched him walk out of the front door of the cottage with his phone in his hand. He took up a post in the gazebo and touched his finger to his phone once he was settled. A half second later, my phone rang in my hand, and I smiled through my anxiety as I answered it.

"You could have just waited to talk to me until tomorrow," I said, keeping the curtains slightly parted so that he couldn't see me if he looked up. He'd wanted to wait until tomorrow, so he could wait until tomorrow. However, that didn't mean I had to go without my eyes on him, even if it was from a much farther distance than I would have preferred.

"No, I was up pacing the kitchen and hoping that Amelia didn't come out and ask me what was wrong, so it's good to get out. I don't have any answers for her, and you know how she dives in hard if I won't tell her what she wants to know."

"I do," I said, thinking of someone else who was a lot like that, too. I kept the thought to myself, though. "I'm concerned about everything going on. I get that my mom said it was magic that created that episode in Mena and not poison, but my mind keeps circling as to who would have done that, and what was the purpose of it? Were they trying to make my whole family sick? Did they think I would be the one who ate the chocolate? Why now? And why leave them at the flower shop where Emma died, under what we're being told are natural circumstances, but I just don't think I can believe that now."

"That's a lot running through your mind."

"It is, but the biggest thing is that I'm afraid I'm not leaning into this being a bad thing because I'm selfish and want my wedding to go off tomorrow without any hitches. Anything else can be dealt with, after, and that feels like I'm a bad person."

"Roxy, you are so very far from a bad person that it's bigger than whatever chasm the note was talking about earlier. The fact that you're even worried about it, despite being told it was a natural occurrence, and just a horrible coincidence of events, means you are a far better person than most people."

"You're just saying that because you're biased." I fiddled with the edge of the curtain, wishing I could be fiddling with the collar of his hoodie instead.

"I won't say I'm not biased, because I completely am, but I've also been around a lot of people who are horrible, so I have a bigger spectrum to put you on, and you are far from the edge. Promise. Anyway, the thing is, ultimately, this is a job for the police. And if Micah and Norm are satisfied it was not murder, then we should be, too. I understand wanting to make sure, but Norm also told you to go get married and enjoy your day. He would never have said that if they really thought there were bad vibes about the way she died."

"You're not wrong."

He chuckled. "Thank goodness you didn't say I was right, or the whole universe might have crashed down on my head through the gazebo. I'd have to get a t-shirt commemorating this occasion and have a plaque put up, since it might never happen again."

"Such the joker." I laughed, too, knowing he was just trying to make everything better, as he always did, and this time I was willing to let him.

"And soon-to-be husband." He yawned. "I promise that if I, or anyone, truly thought something bad had happened to Emma, we'd be in the middle of things. But the professionals are looking into it. The thing with Mena is a whole other issue, of course, and one that your family will have to look into, but I think it can wait another eighteen hours now that she's back to herself. Besides, everyone is on notice about it now and will make sure that we're all safe. Let's get through the 'I do,' and then we'll go from there."

"Have I told you today that I love you?"

"I recall a time or two those words came out of your mouth, but I'm not against being an overachiever if you want to say it again."

"I love you."

"Luckily, I love you, too. Now let's go to sleep. We've got a big day tomorrow, and a lot of people to impress with our amazing recitation of vows, and fabulous dancing on that floor they're bringing up in the morning. I'm going to need you sharp and sassy for tomorrow, so people know you're actually serious about being with me forever and not just settling for the one guy who was smart enough to think you're awesome."

"You're laying it on a little thick there, Mr. Winchester."

"Not at all, soon-to-be-Mrs. Winchester. It's just the right amount of admiration and devotion to someone whom I had no idea I needed in my life until I found her."

There was something to watching him down in the gazebo, gripping the back of his neck as he talked to me, knowing he meant every word.

"I really do love you so much. I'm forever grateful you came here to escape things and instead decided to get involved in other things," I said.

"And if anyone had told me my life would be filled with magic, and family, and you two years ago, when I was running here to hide, I would have never believed them." He glanced up toward the window where I was standing and smiled, even as he averted his eyes quickly. "Tomorrow is just a continuation of what we're building, but I really appreciate you being in for the whole shebang. I know you wanted something far less complicated, but at least you were able to get Sharon to take on some of the burden. So, let's enjoy the fruits of her labor tomorrow, and then we can be off and running on all the other things that make up our life."

"Deal," I kissed two of my fingers and placed them on the glass as we said goodbye. Then I watched him walk back into the little cottage where his family now resided after they'd been estranged for years. And now he'd be moving in here, and his family and my family would be in what could almost be considered a compound, which was just fine with me. I loved having everyone around in a way that I had never thought I would, since I was the one who remained stationary while everyone else jaunted off to far-flung places. But now, we'd all be here together, and that made me happy.

Okay then. So, we just needed to get through tomorrow without any trouble, and then we'd be off and running.

This time, I did knock on the wooden window frame to not jinx myself. I only hoped the universe heard my calling and answered it in my favor.

Chapter 7

The day of my wedding dawned bright and early, but I did not look like a spring chicken when I faced myself in the mirror. Despite having talked with Dean and feeling slightly better about the situation after we hung up, it had come back to haunt me during the witching hour. I'd tossed and turned the rest of the night, never fully falling back to sleep.

We had set the wedding for the morning hours so we could do a lunch afterward. That way, we'd have the rest of the night to start unboxing Dean's things and just enjoy our first evening as Mr. and Mrs. Winchester. I even had a whole crock pot thing in the galley kitchen put together to cook throughout the day. Nothing like pre-planning in an effort to stay in and separate ourselves from anyone else for just twelve or so hours. Well, at least until tomorrow morning, when we planned on having family time before everyone left the next day.

Eyeliner in hand, I pulled my eyelid taut to be able to get the wings I'd been practicing for the last month.

As I lined, my mind wandered. It could just be a coincidence that the chocolates carried what sounded like a curse. They were labeled for us, and next to my flowers in the store, sure. But if no one else had touched them, and there were no others, then anyone else should be fine.

Except, what if they weren't the only box in the store? And what if Emma had eaten one, but had no one to save her like my mother? Where had they come from in the first place? I hadn't ordered anything like them and had originally just thought Emma was gifting them to us for the inconvenience of having to pick up my flowers, instead of having them delivered.

But I didn't know that for sure.

Using the eyeliner and a white tissue, I began writing down my questions. I probably wouldn't be able to read them after the wedding, but I wasn't going to forget that I wanted some answers and the gist of what I was looking for. I also needed to get them out of my head and down on something. If I didn't, I was going to end up obsessing about them when I should have been obsessing about meeting my man under an arch where we would swear our lives and love to each other for all our days on the earth and after.

Switching to the other eye, I masterfully flicked the eyeliner out beyond the end of my lid to create a beautifully swooped wing. That was better, and with the eyes done, I could focus on the rest.

I had asked to be left alone for the first part of the morning to prepare myself with some of the basics. Since I couldn't get into the dress myself, I had deliberately left it downstairs in the first-floor rooms. I'd made sure it was still okay last night after Taboo had been in there with it, but it was perfect, and so was the dog. We hadn't heard from Rick about picking up his companion, but Poobah was fine with keeping the dog for a little while longer. I expected the dog would come with Poobah today for the wedding, and we'd put him back in the rooms downstairs during the ceremony. That was the plan, anyway.

And by then, I'd already have the dress on. I'd also left it down there so that I didn't have to try to walk down two flights of stairs in heels with a wedding train, just in case I stumbled and landed at the bottom of the stairs, seriously injured or dead. For that very reason, Anjanetta, my older sister, had made me a monogrammed dressing robe with my initials embroidered on the back and the pocket. I donned that now because everything I could do up here had been done up here.

I considered dropping my phone into the deep pocket on my hip, but then thought better of it. I did not need the distraction, and I'd be coming back up here after the ceremony, but before the reception kicked off, to change out of the big dress and downsize it for something I wasn't afraid to take a twirl around the dance floor in.

Hesitating a second, I almost turned back at the top of the stairs and called Norm about my thoughts, but I stopped myself and started down the stairs in my bedroom slippers. He did not need me. And he would do the right thing if he thought there was anything wonky about Emma's death.

I had to trust him on that, since it was his job, not mine, and he was very capable of doing it.

Onward to the wedding!

There was much "oohing" and "ahhing" as I stepped into the ultimate decadence I'd ordered online, and had Millie, the seamstress in town, alter to fit me. My mom kept wiping her eyes, and I had to stop her from reaching out to touch the cream-colored dress because her mascara was running.

"I don't remember you crying this much at Anjanetta's wedding. I hope those are happy tears," I said, handing her a tissue for the third time in five minutes. Maybe I should have taken my chances with the stairway and a wedding train. Choo-choo instead of boo-hoo...

"I'm just so excited about this whole thing, and it's been thirty-five years today since I picked out my own dress for my wedding, so I guess I'm a little nostalgic."

I immediately felt like a jerk. I was the farthest thing from a bridezilla as you could be, but this whole Emma thing was keeping me unbalanced, and I needed to let it go so I could sink into the present and not just think about getting to the end. Norm knew what he was doing, and me ruining my own wedding was not going to help with anything.

"Sorry, my mind keeps going back to things it shouldn't be worrying about today." I took a deep breath, or as deep as possible, considering I was trussed up like a turkey in the corset top that had seemed like a good idea when I had said yes to the dress, but now felt a little like being swaddled when I wanted to run free.

"It's okay. This is your big day. It should be about you."

I grabbed her hand and pulled her in for a hug. "It's about all of us, and I want it to go as well as possible. Even if there's a slip up or two, as long as I say 'I do' and so does Dean, it will be perfection."

And then it was. I walked out through the dining room's French doors to the yard in full bloom. Guests sat in wooden folding chairs we'd pulled out of the shed, and they all stood and turned to watch me walking down the aisle on the arm of my father, who was dressed like we were in the high society of Victorian times. It fit him, and I watched as my mom cocked an eyebrow at him and blew him a kiss. Then that was the last thing I looked at as I caught Dean's gaze and held on for the entire length of my walk. His eyes were wide and his smile wider. He rubbed his hands together, rolled his shoulders, and then pulled on the pointed edges of his vest, done in purple and green paisley brocade. Moose sat on the toe of one of his shiny shoes, watching the procession with little to no interest.

This man was everything I could ever want, and my steps quickened a little when I realized how close I was to truly being his wife.

Dad tugged on my elbow and huffed out a laugh. "I promise he'll still be there if we follow the rhythm of the song for our walk. He's not going to run. You've got that boy under a spell of the very best kind. Enjoy the stroll, my darling."

I slowed down, and Dean's smile got wider, which I wouldn't have thought was possible.

When we got to the gazebo, my dad kissed me on the cheek and put my hand in Dean's, then slapped him on the back. "She's all yours now!"

The crowd laughed, and we got down to the business of saying "I do."

I couldn't really tell you what happened after those words. I know we were supposed to light a candle together and then mix sand. We also tied a knot in a white rope he'd pulled from the ferry shed, and then we kissed as a married couple for the first time. The kiss was no different physically from any number of kisses we'd had over the last year, but the feeling was different. And when we pulled apart, there was a sparkle in Dean's eyes that would have rivaled the fireworks the books put out when they had something important to share with me.

Everyone clapped, but no one louder than Sharon, who stood off to the side as the wedding planner, ensuring everything went as she'd planned, check-marking her way down one of her many lists. I would thank her later for making sure all the parts and pieces were in place, so I could concentrate on just the one detail I needed to happen and then did without a single hitch.

That's when the dancing started. Well, first I threw the bouquet, and as had been previously planned, everyone stepped back at the same time to make sure Mena caught it. She almost didn't because of my faulty and clumsy throw, but three of the other women on the dance floor with her played a game of keep the object in the air by batting it away from them and toward her.

When she caught it, she put her nose in the blooms and had eyes only for Micah, who was standing on the edge of the dance floor with his arms crossed over his chest.

We'd set up a thing where he would be the one to catch the garter when Dean tossed it in a few minutes. Maybe some concessions would be made when they had to dance with each other as the next prospective couple, bringing us to the next wedding of the season.

Mena would have to unbend enough to get over whatever she thought was wrong with their circling each other, but that was a worry for another day. Today, I had no more worries. Everything had happened exactly as it should. The rings, carried down the aisle by my fabulous cat, were safely seated on our hands. Amelia had kept her promise and had not hurled flower petals at anyone at all. I'd watched from behind the curtains in the dining room to make sure. And now, Mena had caught the bouquet.

Fabulous!

Or at least it was fabulous for a second, until I felt a shift in the atmosphere and looked toward the side yard to find Norm standing with his hands stuffed in his pockets and his face arranged into a full-on frown.

Maybe he was here to congratulate me?

Yeah, I didn't think so either.

Chapter 8

I struggled not to think *it was fun while it lasted*. There were, of course, any number of reasons Norm could be here. Maybe our nearest neighbor had complained about the noise level. Maybe Mrs. Lincoln, who lived down by the water, had seen a bird fly over her house and had reported it, and Norm was making the rounds to verify her story.

The problem with either of those was that there was no way they were true, because both people were sitting in the wooden chairs around the corner. So, there could only be one reason Norm was here with that look on his face. It was a look I remembered from the first time we had interacted about a dead body I had found. It wasn't fun that time, and I had a distinct feeling it wouldn't be any more fun this time, either.

Since I appeared to be the only one who had seen him standing off to the side, I quietly slipped away, leaving everyone else performing to some chicken dance song from the fifties.

As soon as I reached his side, he walked away, around the corner of the inn to stand near the stairs leading up to the front porch.

I followed, laughing nervously. "Should I be concerned? Am I in trouble?" Fortunately, I had changed after the vows from the big dress with the corset and the train into a cream-colored brocade dress that swung out from my hips and hit my knees. I was wearing the same shoes, though, since I'd chosen flats at the last second to walk down the aisle.

Norm pinched the bridge of his nose and then ran his hand over his hair. He blew out a breath, and I wanted to shake him and tell him to just spit it out. I'd already said, "I do." That had been my primary goal for today, and it was accomplished. Anything else was peanuts compared to having that done and over with.

"Come on, Norm. We're friends here, and it's my wedding day. Just tell me whatever you need to tell me, and let me get back to the horrible dance that's happening right now before they play that Macarena thing." I sounded desperate when I really didn't want to, but he wasn't talking, only heavily sighing and rubbing his forehead.

"I don't know if you're aware, but we have a new chief at the station."

"Okay." I drew out the word, not sure where he was going with this.

"And he has ideas, and no real knowledge of how our town works. I'm sure he's just trying to cover all his bases, but he wants to talk with you about Emma's death."

"I answered all the questions you asked at the florist shop. You said that it was all clear-cut." My mind was racing, though, because why would a chief want to talk with me? Did it have to do with this not just being a heart attack, and instead my fear that it was actually a murder was true? I should have knocked on the freaking wood when I thought that last time.

"He's saying there are inconsistencies." Norm did the air quotes around that last word, and my stomach dropped into my flats.

"Can it wait until tomorrow? I'd really like to have this day be untarnished by anything having to do with murder."

But he was already shaking his head. "He wants you down at the station as soon as possible. He was going to come arrest you, but I managed to talk him into letting me come and get you instead, especially because I have to bring Micah back with me also. Apparently, we're both about to get a dressing down like we've never seen before."

"Why?"

"Because we should have treated this like a crime scene from the beginning, per the new chief, and the fact we didn't means we now have to be reactive instead of proactive. To say the least, he is very unhappy." Norm shrugged his narrow shoulders. "I don't think you had anything to do with this, and I'm still not convinced it's anything but a natural death, but I have to do things his way. I'm really sorry about this, but at least it's better than having some squad of guys pull up and yank you out of the wedding. Is it winding down?"

It was, but then my life was just supposed to be starting as the newly beringed Mrs. Winchester, not a possible suspect of a murder.

"I'm going to have to tell someone where I'm going." I dropped my chin to my chest and shut my eyes. Damn. I was going to cry, and I almost never cried.

"Hey, it's okay," Norm said, putting a hand on my shoulder.

Sucking in a breath, I forced myself to hold back the tears at all costs. "I sure hope so. Has anyone spoken with Rick about any of this?" I asked, knowing that he still hadn't picked up Taboo, who was currently inhabiting the downstairs room, since Poobah hadn't wanted to leave him at his house without some kind of supervision.

"Rick has been in the hospital since last night. When we finally found him at the campground, he started hyperventilating and then passed out. We think it was a panic attack, but then he was talking gibberish, and the EMTs felt it would be better to have him taken to the emergency room, just to make sure he's okay. They kept him overnight because they couldn't get him to settle down. I probably shouldn't be telling you that, but I need to warn you, Roxy, things are weird about this one. The chief seems to have something to prove. Be very careful about how you answer any questions he poses to you."

Now, I was scared and desperately wanted to hide behind Dean. Dean, whom I had to tell I was being taken in for questioning instead of spending the afternoon with him putting up all his books and art and shelving his meager kitchen gadgets. Damn.

But then I felt his presence around the corner, and he cleared his throat as he approached us.

"There a problem here, *officer*?"

I had never heard Dean use that particular tone of voice, and apparently neither had Norm, because his eyes widened before he cleared his throat.

"I've been ordered to bring Roxy in for some questioning."

"And you didn't take into account that it's her special day, and she shouldn't be bothered with something that had nothing to do with her?"

Norm's ears flamed red, and I put a hand on Dean's sleeve. His forearm was as hard as a rock with his fist clenched so tight his knuckles were pale.

"He's doing the best he can, Dean. The new chief wanted to send in a SWAT team, and Norm talked him into just letting him come down and escort me to the station for a few questions. Maybe he just needs to get clarity on what I was doing in the shop, or how I think the door might have been locked, even though it was open when I came in, and I wasn't the one who locked it, and no one else came in behind me that I know of."

Yes, I was totally placating him and babbling while trying hard to sell that story for all I was worth, even though I felt in my bones this was anything but bland. I'd heard Norm's warning, and I was taking it seriously, but I didn't want Dean to be upset until there was something concrete to be upset about.

"I'm coming with you. I'll let Caper know, and he can handle the rest of the reception. We were about to close up after the last dance anyway."

Norm shook his head, but I turned pleading eyes on him and tried to silently communicate that this was the best deal he was going to get out of my new husband. He'd better just take it instead of trying to fight back.

Dean took his phone out of his pocket and tapped in a text, presumably to Caper, then he hooked his arm in mine and led the way to his car. No taking the van with the inn's logo on it to sit in the police station's parking lot. I was fine with that. It was bad enough that I had to show up in my traveling wedding dress when I wasn't supposed to be traveling anywhere.

Dean slit his eyes and stared Norm down the entire time he was handing me into the passenger side of his car, and then he kept his gaze trained on the back of Norm's police car the whole way there. I gently laid my hand on his forearm again, and it was as bunched this time as it had been last time.

"There is no need to choke the steering wheel, dear husband of mine. It's just a few questions, and I did nothing wrong, so I have nothing to fear."

"I don't believe that, and I don't think you really do either. You're just telling me that so I'll calm down. I'm going to be really honest when I tell you it's not going to work today. Maybe other times it has, and it will again, but not right now. I have a bad feeling in the pit of my stomach over this. And it's not going to go away until we're driving away from the police station. So please don't expect me to act like everything is okay."

"Of course." I took the rest of the two minutes of our trip to the station to fill him in on what Norm had told me about his own feelings on this thing. It didn't make Dean any less tense, but his clamped-together lips might be in our favor, so he didn't start anything when we entered the building.

I had, of course, been in here before, as a child when they were doing career days, and it was visit-the-local-police day. I'd also had my fingerprints taken when I was young to have on record, in case anything ever happened.

I had even been in here before to answer questions Norm had and provide any information I might have seen in previous murders that had happened at or around the inn. All this to say, I wasn't a stranger here. But something felt very off as I entered the brick building. Dean must have felt it, too, because he went from walking behind me to moving directly to my side and holding my hand tightly.

"No matter what is said, do not admit to anything," he leaned down and whispered.

"I have nothing to admit because I did nothing wrong," I whispered back.

"I know you've found Norm irritating before, but there's something about the atmosphere here that's telling me this is a whole different animal you're going to be dealing with."

I wiped my sweaty palm against my hip, hoping he was wrong, and we just felt off about stuff because we should be dancing, or unpacking, or maybe both, and instead we were here in the police station with no real reason why.

Norm led us to a bench outside a closed office door. All the blinds on the glass walls were pulled, and there was even a sign on the door itself that said, "Stay Out."

Well then. I would be happy to stay out, but I had a feeling that was not an option.

Especially when a short and hefty guy with a thick mustache yanked open the door and then stood there with his hands on his gun belt, staring me down from ten feet away. There was definite malevolence in his demeanor, and he wasn't even trying to hide it.

I should have asked Aunt Hellen for a charm of protection before I left. But I hadn't, so now I'd just have to deal with this my own way.

So, I rose from the bench and smiled, while holding out my hand like we were old friends meeting for coffee. He completely ignored it, but did grunt at me and jerk his head to the left in a sign that I guessed meant I should follow him. I most certainly did not want to do that, but I didn't really have a choice.

As Dean and I started walking in his direction, I grabbed a pamphlet about neighborhood safety when I passed the counter and prayed I wouldn't have to use it, but was thankful I had it, just in case.

"Remember, you didn't do anything." I would have assigned those words to Dean, but it was definitely Norm's voice that whispered to me as he walked the other way down the hallway. I turned my head to follow his progress out to the front, but he never looked back.

The big guy in front of us trundled down the hallway as if on a mission, and I was afraid that mission was destroying me, though I didn't know why. Norm had asked questions. I'd offered answers beyond even what he'd asked. I didn't have a part in this whole thing, other than finding poor Emma.

When he got to an interrogation room—that's what it was called right on the door—he shoved the door open roughly, then held it open for me to pass him. But as soon as Dean tried to follow, the chief stepped in front of him and broke the connection between our hands. That loss was far more significant than I would have thought.

"I'm only talking to her. You wait outside."

"Absolutely not," Dean said, trying to muscle his way into the room with me.

"We do this my way, or we do it the harder way. Either's fine with me, but I warn you that you won't like what I'll do to keep you out of this room."

I just wanted to get this over with. I had done nothing wrong, and starting a pissing match right now would not serve any purpose, except to make the chief even more aggressive. I was in a safe place, and there were red lights of cameras blinking from the three corners I could see.

I waved the pamphlet at Dean and shook my head behind the chief's back. I was not without protection, just in case.

"I'll be right outside the door, Roxy," he finally said after about five seconds.

"Smart choice, surprisingly," the chief said, and then slammed the door in Dean's face.

The clank of the door startled me enough to make me jump a little. I hid it by seating myself at the metal table on the far side of the room. I placed the pamphlet under my thigh on the chair and prepared for whatever battle we were going to have here. The cameras would be on, if nothing else, and I could yell like nobody's business if I had to.

The chief turned around and planted his hands on his side of the table.

"Now that I've got you..." he said menacingly, and all the blinking lights went dark.

Chapter 9

Normally, I was not one to panic. I'd been through a lot over the years, even during my sheltered inn life. This man could not do anything to me without some serious repercussions, and I was going to have to bank on that while playing this very smart.

I just hoped I had it in me to replace the shaking that had started in my toes and was moving up my legs with something more confident. I clamped my hands together on the table and waited to see what came next.

"Nothing to say?" he said snidely. "That's interesting. I'm told you always have a lot to say about a lot of things." He plunked himself down in the chair opposite me, then leaned forward with his elbows planted on the table and his hands clasped in the air, as if he were going to bring those fists down on me like a wrecking ball. He could certainly try. I didn't have much talent outside of the book reading and the sparkling letters of doom, but that didn't mean I was weak. He would very quickly find that out if he tried anything stupid.

"I choose mainly to talk to intelligent people when given a choice. Since I have no choice at this moment, I'll wait to see what you have to say before crafting a response."

He chuckled, but it had an edge to it that reminded me of those horror movies I used to adore in my teen years. "See now, it's very interesting also that you use the word 'crafting' when you say that. Not many people use that word anymore, unless they're of a certain persuasion."

That made absolutely no sense to me. What persuasion was he talking about? I chose to keep my lips sealed this time and waited to see what other stupidity he was going to go with next.

"Your people were all about talking themselves up back in the day, or didn't you know that?"

My people? What on earth was he talking about? Again, I would wait to ask, though. He needed a little more rope to hang himself with before I said anything. Plus, he hadn't asked a question yet, so I had nothing to answer.

He might be menacing, but I didn't truly feel like he could do anything to hurt me. He was a lot of bluster without a lot of action. Sitting and waiting for him to get his story together and actually ask a question or two was probably my best path at this point, and I was going to trust my intuition this time.

He got up to pace on the other side of the table with his one hand clamped around the wrist of the other behind his back. If he were a cartoon character, I was positive there would have been steam pouring out of his ears, and the top of his head would have blown off by now.

I'd wait to see if any of that happened.

Crossing my ankles under the table, I moved my hands to my lap and continued waiting for his next move.

And that move was to pull out the chair across from me, blow out a putrid breath I would have winced at if I was willing to give him any reaction, which I wasn't, and slap his hand on the metal table, causing a clanging sound that also might have made me wince, but I was too taken in by the glint in his eyes. What did he think he had on me, and when was he going to just spill it so I could get out of here? I had done nothing wrong I had nothing against Emma, and I was a good, paying customer with no issues. All I had done was to have found her dead, called the police, taken her dog, and my flowers, home.

Yes, there had been some kind of dark magic on the box of chocolates I'd also taken home, but I certainly wasn't going to tell him that. Not at this point.

"Aren't you going to talk?" His voice started edging toward a whine, and I was fascinated by the way he melted from big tough guy to a child who wasn't getting their toy back just yet.

I simply stared at him, waiting for whatever revelation he thought he had that required me to sit in this stupid room, with this stupid man, with the stupid cameras off.

He snorted. "My mom told me you're all losers, and I shouldn't even try to get you to actually confess to any wrongdoing. That it would be easier to just set a trap and let you trip right into it. I still think I'm the right one on this subject, though."

I shrugged, and his eyebrows went up, while his mouth flattened into a concrete line.

I'd dealt with guests at the inn who had more piss and vinegar over a soufflé that fell before they'd had a chance to get the perfect selfie to post on social media.

"Come on!" he yelled. And the worse he got, the calmer I got. He had nothing. This was all just intimidation, meant to make me cower and tell him whatever he wanted to hear so that I could escape.

"Fine. You want to know what this is?"

That was a question, finally, but I had a feeling it was rhetorical and would benefit me far more to let him just get his rant over.

"This is me finally taking action against you people who think that we're less than you, and who send us packing, even though we did nothing wrong."

Again, with the *you people*. I almost asked him to explain what exactly that meant, but stopped myself before I opened my mouth.

"I know all about you and your 'talents' and the way you use them as if they're just all yours and no one else's. I know all about how you shut us out, and laugh at us, and make us out to be fools because we have the blood, but not the blessings. And if you think I'm going to let you walk away from this murder that I know you committed, then you are very badly mistaken and will pay twice the price than if you'd just admitted it and stop being so freaking uppity."

His choice of that last word nearly startled me into laughing, but I kept that behind my teeth, too. My mind was running rampant with everything he'd said, and I couldn't settle on any one thing to address first, but then he continued.

"How is it that you've found four dead bodies now—*Four*—and yet you've never really been considered a suspect? You're no Jessica Fletcher, who really should have been considered a serial killer, too, and even if she didn't do anything, I know that this is the one I can nail you for. Norm has gone soft on you, and I've been brought in to make sure that does not happen again. I get you off the street and out of the public where you can't do any harm, and maybe you'll trade a thing or two to get yourself out of this mess that you created, or should I say crafted?"

Wow. WOW. *WOW*.

This was...this was a whole other level of wow, and I didn't have any words at the moment to truly explain how I felt beyond shocked. Was he saying his family had our talented blood, but was unable to access the talents that should have been inherent to them? I had never heard of that before. But I wasn't going to ask him to explain because I had better-informed people at home, for far less aggression. And hopefully some concrete answers. First, though, I had to get out of here in one piece.

"Crafted is probably not the best choice of words. Your mother should have told you that, too," I finally managed to say, and it came out far more solid than I had expected. Good.

"Smug."

"Not smug, serious. And I'm just as serious about the fact that whatever grudge you're holding against my family and me, you should let it go. I had nothing to do with any murders, and I was told very specifically that Emma's death was of natural causes. Now, I have a question for you. What do you have that suggests otherwise? And a second one, why on earth would you think it was me who would want to take her out when I know that there were several others who had far more motive than I ever would?"

He had the gall to laugh, sinisterly, derisively, irritatingly. "How do you know there are others who would want her gone? You doing that sleuthing thing again just so that you can get out of yet another murder that has not only happened near you, but I think you did them all?"

"I had nothing to do with any of them." I spread my hands on the table to keep myself anchored.

"And yet you solved every single one and handed them to Norm on a silver platter every time." He quirked a bushy, dark eyebrow at me. "You're just that smart? Or are you just that manipulative? Because I have a list of the talents that have come down through the centuries. My great-grandmother kept that list up to date as much as she could, and there are quite a few of those talents that can make people look the other way, or sway them toward a theory or person you want to be blamed. How do I know that you aren't doing just that?"

He had a list and thought I fit the bill. This was not good in any way, shape, or form, considering that my own family had access to several of the talents he was talking about. I knew in my soul that none of them had used any of them to pin a murder on someone who hadn't confessed to doing it on their own, but I couldn't say that.

"We're done here," I said instead of defending myself or my family. "You've asked nothing that you can put in the record, which is why I believe you shut off the cameras when you slammed the door. And if you truly had any evidence that I'd done anything wrong, you would have started with that, or at least presented some proof you're not just grasping at straws because you have some serious resentment about the place your family finds themselves in. Did they do it to themselves? Did they misstep so badly that they can't be trusted with things that should be natural to them, and yet they can't harness it because someone above us knows it would be used for crime and punishment instead of doing good? Only you, and what you believe in, can answer that, and I'm neither of those things." I stood up in my flats and my creamy white dress that was supposed to have been displayed at my own party, instead of sitting in this hellhole. Walking past him and hoping that he didn't try to manhandle me took far more courage than I would have believed I had in me, but I did it anyway.

He slammed his hands down on the table again when I knocked on the door to be let out. He could ramble and rage all he wanted, but I was not going to put myself in his sphere where I had to be witness to it.

There was a click of the doorknob, and then Shirleen stood there with stark concern on her face. With her red hair and pink fitted skirt and jacket, she was normally full of joy, even when she was doing the hard work of listening to people panic and figuring out what they needed for help. Right now, though, she was frowning, but that frown was aimed over my shoulder where the chief—I hadn't even gotten his name yet—sat without moving.

"Thank you," I said as I stepped around her and left the room that was absolutely seething with hate and menace. He was what was wrong in the air around here. He had coated every square inch of this place with his negativity. He was not going to do that to me, too.

The other times I'd looked into the murders, I had been serious about finding the culprit for a variety of reasons. And yet I'd also enjoyed the chase a little, thought it was interesting and fascinating to follow the clues from place to place to find who would think that there was no alternative to what their issues were, except to kill someone.

This time was going to be different. This time, I had the same motivation, but I also had a new one. I was taking down this chief no matter what I had to do to make that happen. I had a feeling he was very aware of that as I left him in the room, and Shirleen closed the door, leaving him in there with his hate and his anger.

Game on, but it wasn't a game this time. It was truth-seeking that would have far more to do with making sure that there were no holes in the case I was going to present to the station, one that there was no way he could weasel out of.

So then maybe not game on, but maybe it was more come and get me. Because I was going to prove without a shadow of a doubt it was not me and could never be me. But I was also going to prove to him that he was not only wrong, but he and his stupid resentment were dead wrong. I looked forward to seeing him squirm when it was all said and done.

I took that resolve with me as I walked along the hallway back to the front desk. I took it with me, too, when Norm stopped me with a soft hand on my forearm.

"You okay?" he asked, checking me out from head to toe. For bruising? For despair? For fear?

"Absolutely, but do not under any circumstances ask me not to look into this one." I couldn't tell him everything that had been said in that room, since it would divulge too many things Norm was not supposed to know. But I could do one thing to make the chief uncomfortable. "What is this guy's name?"

"Grady Morony. Chief Morony."

I choked on the laughter that wanted to come bursting out of me. I cleared my throat instead. "Seriously?"

"Very seriously."

"And no one sees that irony in that?"

He half-smiled. "Oh, a lot of us do, but we don't say anything because he's the boss."

"Well, he's not the boss of me, so brace yourself because I'm not going away until this goes away. Understand?"

"Completely. And best of luck. I don't think I'm going to be able to help much, or share anything really, because I don't want to lose my job, but I will be looking into things over on my side with everything I've got."

"I trust you," I said and then walked to where Dean was sitting in the waiting room, looking like he was about to burst out of his seat.

"You okay?" he asked, and almost made me cry.

"I will be." I stiffened my upper lip and my resolve along with my spine. I'd come through with the real culprit three other times. This time would be no different, especially since there was far more at stake this time than any time before.

Chapter 10

After hauling our tails out of the police station—dignified, but still in quick time—I marched back into the inn like a girl on a mission, because I was. Everyone had dispersed when the party was over, per Aunt Hellen. Sharon had left me a message begging me to look into her friend's murder. I'd call her back later.

Dean's phone dinged next to mine, and it was Aunt Hellen responding to him, letting her know we were on our way back. She'd brought everyone back in to congregate again in the dining room, where there was space enough for all of us, including those who did not have or did not know about our talents.

I was going to have to be careful about what I said and how I said it with so many people in the room, but I could do that. I'd save the bigger, more menacing stuff for when it was just family. Which included Dean and his brood by marriage now. Together, all of us would make this happen, come hell or even hot water.

"Where did you go off to?" Glennis asked, carrying out cookies for the crowd around the table. Of course, she was going to feed us. That was how her whole world worked. "You didn't even get to eat your cake, and you'd been waiting for that thing for months."

The cake...I had been waiting a very long time for that, but I'd just get another piece later, hopefully. "Was there any left?" I asked.

"There wouldn't have been if it were up to those two." She pointed a finger at Caper and Isaac, who both bowed their heads as if in shame. And yet their shoulders were shaking, and I heard a low, but distinguishable snicker come from their direction. "I saved you a piece before they could devour it all."

Both of the men's heads popped up, as if they might go on the hunt for the cake. But they didn't have to look or sniff far, because while Glennis had a tray of cookies in one hand, she also had a small plate of cake in the other. And that was the one she delivered to me with two forks.

"You think I'm sharing this with anyone?" I asked, pulling the plate closer to me as I wrapped my whole arm around it. Someone would think I was building a barrier that no one could or would want to cross. Someone would not be wrong.

"I think it might be nice if you at least feed one bite to your husband. We didn't get to see if you decided to smash it in each other's faces or not. That's my favorite part of any wedding." Glennis stepped back, but kept watch over me and my cake.

"You hate people destroying food." I took up my fork, even as I silently squealed in glee over the word husband and perused how much of the piece of cake I was going to devour first.

"Smashing cake is not destroying it, and to be honest, I get the biggest kick out of people trying not to waste it by not wiping it off with a napkin, instead using their fingers to make sure they don't have to throw any of it away. Now, share it with your husband, and then tell me if it lives up to the hype."

I had heard about the red velvet cake with a wonderfully creamy, vanilla filling on social media weeks ago, but I had never been able to get any of our previous guests to commit to it. They'd had other desserts they wanted for their special occasions. I would never have tried to do it myself because I was not a very good cook. This thing looked amazing, though, and I had every belief that it would taste just as wonderful. Especially with the way Caper and Isaac were salivating down the table.

I dipped my fork into the southwest corner of the divine, and then caught Dean's expression in my peripheral vision. Darn him, and his puppy dog eyes. He had come with me from the beginning, so he hadn't gotten any cake, either. No matter how much I wanted all this cake to myself, I couldn't just leave him without the dessert when Glennis really had cut me a big piece. Probably more than I could actually eat, but oh, how I wanted to eat it all.

I moved the fork from in front of my mouth to aim it at Dean's mouth. I held my hand under it just in case he dropped any. I didn't want it to go to waste on the tablecloth.

But he expertly took the morsel off the fork and nodded at me as he hummed low in his throat.

I took my own bite and knew exactly the reason for that humming. The spongy and thick cake was divine, like nothing I had tasted before, and I very quickly marked it as the one thing we'd have every anniversary. Dean's reaction to the cake told me this wouldn't even have to be a discussion.

But enough about the cake, though I did take one more bite before I put my fork down and prepared myself for telling what I could to this crowd. The extra stuff would only be heard by those who knew all of me and shared my talents.

"First of all, thank you to everyone for covering the end of the wedding and seeing all our guests off." The reception had included many of the locals, even Mrs. Lincoln and her dog. I had completely cut out on my duties to thank everyone for celebrating this day with me, but I would cover that by sending out thank-you cards. "It was completely unexpected, but I wanted to let you all know what's happening because we're about to start a full-out mission, and I have a feeling I'm going to need everyone's help on this."

Glennis shot me a look, and so did my mom. Both motherly looks, and it occurred to me how much of my childhood and teenage years, along with the last ten years, I had been mothered by Glennis, while my mother was out on the road with my father. That meant a lot to me, and I appreciated her and everything she'd done, even when she was a pain in my rear end. And right now, I needed to protect myself and my family, those who shared my blood, those who were mine through marriage, and those who were here by helping create this inn. Because this chief was not only coming after me, but he was also coming for my whole world, and he'd have to fight every single one of us to take that down.

I looked around the table, and I was never prouder of the people I'd surrounded myself with. But I was about to challenge them, and as much as I would have liked to do this completely on my own and not involve them, I knew there was no way I could do that and win.

"There's a new chief in town, and he appears to have it out for me." I left it at just me because the fact that he was out for my whole family needed to only be shared with my actual family, including the Winchesters, of which I was now one. My porters, cleaning crew, and kitchen staff were not at the center of this at all, but by working for me, they were on the periphery and deserved to know as much of what was going on as I could share with them.

"Let me at 'em," Malcolm, one of the porters, said. He was in his seventies, and I'd been told he was a scrapper when he was younger, despite how refined he looked now in his waistcoat.

He brought a smile to my face for the first time in over an hour, and for that, I was so incredibly thankful for him. "You're the best, and I very much appreciate your willingness to take a punch or two, but since he is the police, we're going to have to do this the sneakier way." I took another bite of my cake, and my mom narrowed her eyes at me. I should have finished the whole thing before I ever started this conversation. I wasn't going to be able to take another bite until I got all the information out. As long as Caper didn't reach out with that fork he had in his hands to get another bite, we should be fine.

"Sneakier than the other three times?" Poobah said, and I knew that he knew more than I had said already.

"Yes, sneakier than last time. I'm on this Chief Morony's hit list, and he wants to pin this one on me because he seems to think I'm some kind of serial killer."

There were gasps and a few fists hitting the table, like we were getting ready to do an all-out battle, and I was doing that last holler of encouragement before sending my troops out to the fight.

"I did nothing wrong," I was quick to say. "And there's no evidence he has to prove that I'm lying. He took me into an interrogation room today, though, and shut off the recording, then threatened me, telling me he knew I did it, and he wasn't going to rest until he proved it."

"That seems very vindictive and not at all the way the law is supposed to work, especially from someone who is a leader in the force." Harvey, my other porter, said. He was in his sixties and had spent over twenty years on that same force before he came to me. I could see his temper rising and needed to get him back down off the ceiling, or he'd go to the station and probably take matters into his own hands.

"I'm totally with you on that," I said. "But no matter how much I just want to confront the guy, and make him take back his words, and put down his ridiculous attitude, I really think the better way is going to be for us to all work together. We need to find this killer before he makes the true case that it's me when it most certainly is not." I took a deep breath and used the time to flick my gaze over every person in the room. "Can I ask that you all help me this time? I know I've had you do little errands here and there, or verify information that I had been given or found on my own before. I'm thinking this time it's going to be best if I appear to just keep my head down and not be outwardly involved, but also still be looking for information. Since we don't have guests, other than family, at the moment, we can use the downstairs room that used to be mine to keep all the info in one place. We'll correlate everything there."

A resounding yes met my words, and I was never so grateful for the lovely people who had shown up in my life, from those who were related to those who had chosen to be part of my family.

"Okay, so we're going to need to split things up." I gave out assignments to get in contact with anyone who knew Emma, or had been in her circle, while she'd lived here over the last ten years. I also asked Poobah to get in to see Rick, if at all possible, while he was in the hospital.

"Your aunt is probably a better person to send after him."

I wasn't sure if I should ask him why right now, especially since Poobah was taking care of Taboo, Rick's dog. I'd have to do more investigating on that later.

Instead, I looked over at Aunt Hellen, and she nodded. "I can do that, even if I also didn't like quite a few things about him. I'm more able to hide it. Must be because I'm younger."

Poobah cackled at that, and it relieved the tension in the air that everyone seemed to be trying to work through.

"Look," I said, shaking my head. "I get that this might be very uncomfortable. In theory, he can't pin anything on me that I didn't do. But I'd also like to start out my life as Mrs. Winchester without having to look into every nook and cranny, hoping he's not going to send me up the river to prison, either. So, we do this in pieces, and I keep my head down, while you all ask around to your friends, and not-so-much friends, to find out any dirt."

"Can do!" Caper said, and Isaac flexed his fingers, like he was getting ready to go to town on his computer, just as soon as I released them from the dining room.

"I appreciate it more than I can say, really. You all have been with me for varying amounts of time, but each of you means the world to me. Thank you."

That was the cue for the kitchen staff and the porters to head to their respective homes. Everyone else was housed here in one fashion or another for the time being. We all got up and headed out to the billiard room with Dean and his family hard on my heels, and my own family lagging a little bit behind.

Eventually, I got everyone around the pool table and took up a spot near the dartboard.

"So now what's really going on? What trouble have you managed to get yourself into?" Anjanetta asked. How did I know it was going to be her who fired the first question? Because she was the oldest, that's why.

"I didn't do anything," I responded.

"You always used to say that, and yet somehow you always manage to do something, just not what we expected."

"She has a point," Mena chimed in, and I gave her the stink eye.

"Thanks so much." I stared her down.

"Girls," my mom said. "We are not here to fight, and I don't have enough room or temperament at the moment to give time-outs. Cool it, and let's see what Roxy has to say."

"Thank you."

"Don't thank me until I know how you got yourself in trouble."

The whole room snickered at my mom's words, except for me. But then I remembered the things I used to do, and how I used to try to mimic Mena and get someone else to take the fall, and it just never worked. I snickered, too, but then cut myself off and cleared my throat.

"I think we have some real problems, and I don't know what to do about them. Mom, can you throw a charm to keep anything I say in this room? Right now, I can't afford for anyone else to find out, because I don't have any explanations that don't involve us outing ourselves."

"Oh, that sounds far more serious than I had thought." Mom moved counterclockwise—or widdershins for those who loved words like me—throughout the room into the four corners and cast in each one a protection spell and a banishment of evil. I considered sending her down to the police station to do the same thing, but not yet. I wasn't willing to send her into that lion's den unless I absolutely had to.

"All right, the protections are cast, and you have piqued my interest," Poobah said, standing on the opposite side of the table from me. "Now tell us what really happened at the station."

I had already told Dean in the car on our way back here, so I knew he could fill in any holes if I got so entrenched in what I was saying that I forgot some of the more important parts. That's what husbands were for, right?

So, I told them as much as I could, and Dean added a few parts, along with telling them about the vibe he kept feeling in the waiting room. No one was happy there. He hadn't been in the station much before, but he'd been in other stations, and even with their primary business being keeping the peace and following the law, it was rare that he'd felt that kind of angst from every person walking around in the building.

"So, he's part of a clan that should have talents, but doesn't." Dad took the darts from the dartboard and started hurling them with a precision I envied. I was good, but he had always been better, even after not playing on this board for long periods of time.

"That's the gist of what I got, and he was saying we were to blame for some reason. Also, that we talk too much and do bad things, but think we have the freedom to do it because of our talents." That part had struck me the most. What did he think we did that was cruel or unusual? I was certain that everyone I was related to had never done harm to another, at least not in my lifetime.

"I've never run across anyone like that before, Poobah," Anjanetta said, and Clive nodded his head.

"Neither have I." Mena took up the stool at the marble bar and leaned back against the wall.

We were all still dressed in our wedding finery. I so wanted to be in my pajamas, cuddled up with my new husband in our part of the house, going through tedious amounts of boxes of things that I might have to veto to keep the aesthetic I was going for on the third floor. But that was getting pushed further and further along the timeline.

"There were some people back long ago who had used what they possessed for evil intent," Poobah said. "They were dealt with in a fashion that wasn't explained, but I thought was more of ending the line, not just keeping them bound without powers. Where was that?" he asked no one in particular as he bent down next to Mena and opened the cabinet containing the book of secrets he'd created from the pool table rubbings.

We all stood around not talking as he paged through the book, mumbling to himself. The silence was deafening, and I was about to ask him what on earth was taking so long when he stabbed a finger into one particular page and then frowned.

"Well, that means something totally different from what I had originally thought," he said, and then passed a hand over the book. The words scrambled themselves on the white background like they were ants trying to scurry away and not get trampled on. "We need answers from the book."

"But the letters aren't glowing," I said before I thought my way all the way through that. "Every time something has to do with the murder, the letters have always glowed."

Uncle Vince cleared his throat. "You've often asked it a question or were the one looking for it, though, weren't you? I've never seen a book glow randomly unless you were looking for some kind of answer, even if you didn't say it out loud."

"True enough." I bit my lip, and my mom shook her head at me. I released my lip from my teeth and instead pressed my tongue to the roof of my mouth. "But what should I ask? Is it bigger than Morony?"

"Which is a pretty dead-on name if you ask me," Amelia said.

This child was going places.

"I'm going with my normal ask then. What do I need to know about the murderer or murder?" I placed my hand on the page with the scrambling letters. I didn't know if it would work, since I'd never dealt with something like this, but for it being my first time, I couldn't be appreciative enough that I was surrounded by people I loved and trusted. Especially when the letters started crawling up my arm.

Chapter 11

My first inclination was to shake them off like you would if you found a spider crawling on you. But Poobah grabbed my elbow where the letters had not yet been able to reach and spoke in a language I didn't understand. What couldn't this man do? And why didn't I know all he could do?

I let those questions slide right out of my mind when I felt the letters receding off my arm and landing back on the page, solid again in sentences Poobah had gotten from the pool table many moons ago.

As soon as they all arranged themselves in the right place, the entire book glowed with the power of a thousand suns. I really hoped there was no one passing the door out in the hallway, because I couldn't even imagine the strength of the light that must be shooting out from beneath the door.

Before I could say anything, though, the light faded to a more sedate glow, allowing me to read the words above the book.

Rotting Trees Can Feed the Forest

We all kind of stood there in silence as the letters faded to black and then sprinkled back onto the page, as if they'd never left.

Now, normally, I got what the messages meant if I was reading just from the text on a benign question. The last two answers

I'd received since Emma died had been more cryptic than I was used to, but being aware of a chasm and lies still didn't seem like they would take too much to figure out, once I had a chance to really think about them. This one, though? This was baffling.

"Bueller, Bueller, Bueller...anyone want to take a guess as to what that means?" I asked, figuring no one would jump in, but then Caper tapped his lip as he came up on the book and looked at the original text.

"In folklore, people let the trees that fell stay on the ground, not wanting to remove their spirits from the forest itself, just in case that spirit would follow you and be released if you burned the wood. People would rather cut the trees down, because then you cut off the spirit instead of simply letting it reside in the tree."

"Isn't that a story Mom used to tell us?" Dean asked, looking directly at his brother. I had heard so little about Dean's family outside of the four I knew that I was surprised to think I didn't even know his mother's name, much less who she had been, and what she had believed.

"It is. But hers always came with the caution that if you don't want to take negativity with you, then you have to leave the negativity to rot where it stands. You can't always fix things just by clearing out the brush and mining for the truth."

"Sometimes things you think you need to fix cannot be fixed and need to be left to rot on their own." My mom walked around the table. "It takes a different kind of mind, one you might not want to actually understand, to get why certain people do the things they do." She put her hand on Caper's shoulder. "Your mom was a smart woman."

Caper locked eyes with Dean. "She was."

Dean cleared his throat. "So, we have these messages, and yet, I'm not entirely sure what we're supposed to do with them. If they mean we should let this other faction of non-talented bloodlines just go about their business so they can rot on their own, I don't know that I see that as a good thing to do. Especially in this current situation. This man, at least, is out for us and particularly Roxy. I can't let that stand."

"None of us can," Poobah said, running his finger over the text in the book. "Since I won't take the Rick assignment, why don't you leave me with the book? I'll see if there's information to glean from here. I've read this thing a thousand times. But with this new angle, maybe something will pop out at me I hadn't considered before, or it will show it in a different light than the one I've previously been using to showcase what's in here."

"In the meantime, Roxy, you need to keep that head down." My dad stood next to my mom, but reached out a hand to me. I went to him, and he folded my hand in his, then brought it to his chest to rest near his heart. "You're the stationary one, the rock for a lot of this crazy family, but I think this time you're going to have to let us do some of the work."

I came in closer for a hug, and he wrapped his arms around me.

"Between us, we might be able to do at least half of the work you normally do. Everyone will report back to you, and you can use that writer brain of yours to make all the pieces fit."

My writer brain. I hadn't thought much about that over the last year and a half due to all the goings on around here. I'd been getting this place to run smoothly under new management, dealing with employees who had watched me grow up and not necessarily think of me as a boss, falling in love with Dean and his family, dealing with murders and a ghost I'd never met before. So yeah, I had been doing a lot, but I had also put one of my biggest passions aside to deal with life. Maybe after this was all done, I could get back to penning those stories that I was currently living. But first...

Out of the corner of my eye, I caught a glimmer from the book under Poobah's hand. No one else seemed to be drawn to it, as they were all talking amongst themselves about who was going to do what, and if we should have scheduled check-in times. They wanted to make sure to verify all information was caught and cross-referenced properly in some sort of index that Uncle Vince and Aunt Hellen were putting together.

I left them to it as I inched closer to the book. The glow wasn't an explosion so much as it was a pulsing light, like something you would view through an opaque window. The rhythm was almost hypnotic until I stood right next to my grandfather, and then the light stopped moving and seemed to seep out of the book, creeping across the table as the note from the repair manual had earlier.

It coalesced on the green matting after a few seconds of writhing into place.

A Weary Traveler and the Time is Nigh.

I squinted at the words and tried to come up with anything they could mean. And I came up with nothing.

"What does that say to you?" I asked Poobah, who appeared to be as mesmerized as I was.

"I have no idea. You're the one who's the bibliomancer. Isn't this your purview?"

I shot him a look, but he just shrugged.

"Oh, come on," I said. "You seem to be able to do all kinds of things that I never knew about. Not to mention, you're far older than I am and know more about this book than anyone else. You have to at least have some idea of what it's trying to say."

"Touché on the old joke, nicely done. But the truth is, no, I don't have any idea what this book is talking about. I don't know what it means by a weary traveler, and the time is nigh. What traveler? What time is nigh?" He crossed one arm at his waist and then held onto his opposite elbow as he tapped a finger to his chin.

"And the sentence construction leaves a lot to be desired. Are both the weary traveler and the time nigh? Like both are happening at the same nigh time, or are they separate things to watch out for?"

"That too is a good question, and one you will have time to figure out, I think, while the rest of us run around and do your dirty work." He smiled at me and then kissed me on the forehead. "You have a lot of power in this room, not just because there are talents, but because there's love, and solidarity, and community. We'll get through this, like we have everything else that life has thrown at us."

"Thanks, Poobah."

"Any time, Roxy."

I turned to the room. "All right, it seems we have a few other things to discuss, and then I don't know about you, but I'm exhausted and would like to go to bed."

Mena giggled. "It is your wedding night after all…" And then she winked at me.

I rolled my eyes so hard I almost saw the back of my own skull and gave myself a headache. "You're ridiculous. But it has been a long day, and as for tonight, I'm hoping that we can all get some good rest. Because tomorrow is going to be a kicker. I'll set up a battle station in my rooms down here, and then we'll figure out what comes next once people start bringing in information. At this point, nothing is too big or too small. We need answers, and I know they're out there, if we just ask the right questions."

"We won't let anything happen to you, my dear," Mom said. "No matter if we solve this or not, the cretin down at the station does not have anything that could directly link you to Emma's death. I would, and will, stake my life on that. So, go enjoy your wedding night. Tomorrow will come soon enough."

"Right, and the book just told me that the time is nigh and there's a weary traveler mixed in there somewhere, but hopefully that won't manifest until sometime tomorrow."

Everyone in the room let out a laugh, and the vibe changed. We were going to do this. There was nothing in the world that could stop us because we were linked solidly through blood and through relationships that were iron-clad. I was staking my very life on that and felt good about it.

One by one or as pairs, people started leaving the billiard room. It was like a procession as each of them stopped to hug me or kiss me on the cheek or the forehead. It wasn't like I was saying goodbye, or anything, so I took it as encouragement instead of silent wishes that we weren't here at this moment, and they would indeed see me another day.

Poobah followed the last person out, then it was just Dean and me.

"You know, no matter what happens, we're going to see this through to the end," he said, tugging me into a tight hug and kissing my cheek.

I rested my head against his chest and released a big sigh. "I do know, but I sure would like not to have to do this anymore. It was fun at the beginning, like armchair sleuthing, but I just don't know about making a side hustle out of this. I'd rather not have anyone killed in town anymore, and I'd like the police to be stable enough to do their job, so I don't have to."

"Duly noted. We'll get there."

"You ready to go up?" I asked, knowing I had already unpacked some of his stuff and had made a line of rose petals on the floor to our new bedroom. I had candles to light and chocolates to share, too, but I honestly didn't know if I had it in me at this point to do anything but fall into bed and right to sleep. We had the rest of our lives to eat chocolate and celebrate—as long as I didn't end up in prison, anyway.

We exited the billiard room and turned toward the stairs. We could have taken the back stairs through the kitchen, but that was closed up for the night. Everyone on the second floor was related to me and could easily help themselves, so it wasn't like they were going to pop out of their rooms asking for more towels if they saw us in the hallway or on the stairs.

Dean swept me up in his arms and headed toward the main staircase.

"You are not going to carry me up two flights of stairs." I pushed against his chest and laughed.

"Nope, we're going over to the front door so I can carry you across the threshold. We have to keep up with the traditions that are important."

"And it's important to you to carry me across a threshold? Can't that be upstairs on our new floor?"

"I thought you were sure I couldn't carry you up two flights of stairs."

I pushed against his shoulder, and he pretended to stumble. "I don't want to drop you and have your mom come out to heal you. That's not exactly how I'd like your first night as Mrs. Winchester to go."

Mrs. Winchester. It sounded so dreamy. I laughed and leaned in to kiss him, just as there was a knock on the front door. Once he got an idea, it was hard to dissuade him, and crossing the threshold in his arms sounded like a fairytale, so I would have been fine with that. But a knock on the door could mean anything from I was getting put in jail to someone was in trouble and needed our assistance, or anything in between.

Dean put me down in the foyer, and I straightened my dress before pulling the door open. Standing on the front porch was someone I would not have expected to show up on my doorstep after the sun had gone down, and certainly not looking as done in as she was.

"Mrs. Lincoln? What can I do for you?"

The old woman looked disheveled in a way I hadn't seen her before, even when she was outside trying to bat squirrels away from her precious bird feeders. Her gunmetal gray hair was in curlers, and it looked like she'd thrown on whatever had been handy around her room. The purple pants did not match the vibrant orange house dress she'd paired them with. She hadn't answered me yet, so I almost asked again what she was doing here at the inn and why so late.

Instead, Dean took her hand gently and led her into the foyer. He patted her on the shoulder as he guided her to sit on the bench at the front window.

"Something's obviously wrong, Mrs. Lincoln. What brings you out at this time of the night?"

"I...I..." She hitched in a breath. "I can't find my Fonzy. He got out of the gate twenty minutes ago, and he's not coming back for treats, or the songs I sing him, or the bells he loves."

Fonzy was her ten-pound terror, I meant terrier, who never left her side.

"Did you call the police?" I asked.

She shot me a look, as if I were a complete imbecile.

"No, Roxy, why would I do that when I could just come here first, hoping that you might be able to make him reappear out of thin air?" she scoffed. "Of course, I called the police, but they told me they're too busy to help me. I didn't even get my full concern out to Shirleen before some jerk of a man grabbed the phone and said there were no officers to help with anything unless this had to do with a murder. He wanted to know if I'd seen you around town recently, and if I had, were you doing anything dishonest? He was increasingly rude, so I hung up on him, then came over here because it appears to be your fault he won't help me."

There was so much to unpack there. I wasn't even sure where to start. But first and foremost, find her dog. And for that, I needed Poobah and Taboo.

"Can I get you something to drink while we figure out a game plan to find your dog?"

She narrowed her eyes at me, and I waited. I was not going to beg her to take something from my kitchen. Finally, she nodded.

"I'll take a soda. And don't tell me I can't have it because it's too late or too much sugar." Her whole demeanor was like aggression personified. Probably where Fonzy got it from.

"I would never tell you what you can and can't drink or when, Mrs. Lincoln." I sent a look to Dean, and he headed off to the kitchen. "Now, where did you last see Fonzy, and how long has he been gone?" This, at least, was a mystery I'd much rather try to figure out than the one sitting on the back burner until we could get some more answers. Was that time nigh yet?

Chapter 12

Mrs. Lincoln wasn't much for chatting, at least not with me, so we sat quietly in the lobby as we waited for Dean to return with the soda. What on earth was taking him so long?

I put in a quick text to Poobah, hoping he wouldn't ignore his phone because his favorite game show was on. But he texted me back that he was on his way with Taboo, just as Dean finally came out of the kitchen with a soda as requested. He shot me a look that definitely said we'd talk later. And no matter how much I wanted to ask all my questions now, I waited. Again.

Fortunately, Poobah didn't live far, and once Dean handed over the can of soda, Mrs. Lincoln apparently decided he at least was worth making small talk with. Fine by me.

I stood at the front door, wondering if maybe Fonzy would show up on the porch, having smelled his mistress and wanting to come in the door.

Flummoxed was a word I didn't use often, no matter how much I loved big words. Yet, I couldn't think of another one when I happened to glance over at the porch swing and saw a small dog sitting on the cushions, as if he'd been placed there just waiting for us to find him.

"Mrs. Lincoln," I said, breaking into their conversation.

She huffed at me until she looked up and saw me pointing out through the window. Leaving her soda on the side table, she almost launched herself off the bench and yanked open the front door.

If I'd been given a second, I would have cautioned her against being so aggressive, but she gave me no time. And apparently Fonzy wasn't going anywhere, no matter if he wanted to or not. He appeared to be attached to the porch swing with a kind of chain that I would have associated with racking your bike, like my Uncle Vince did when he brought in donuts.

She was bent over, yanking on the thing, when Dean put a soft hand on her arm, gently removing her, as he talked in a low voice and worked at the chain in a more structured way. It didn't appear to be locked, but loosely knotted.

Who would have done something like that? What was the purpose? Did the person find Fonzy and bring him here? Or had the person been the one to take him in the first place, then brought him to the inn to put yet another layer of angst into this whole episode?

Those were questions for another time and place. Fonzy hadn't made a single sound when Dean was working on freeing him, which surprised me. The terrier was most certainly one of the mouthiest dogs I'd ever met, especially if he was on the other side of the screen door at Mrs. Lincoln's house.

Finally, the little dog was in his mistress's arms, and that was when he started whimpering. Which, of course, was right when Taboo led my grandfather up the stairs from the driveway. Led might have been too gentle a word because it was much more like dragging.

And as soon as Taboo saw Fonzy, they started straining toward each other. In the middle of that strain, Mrs. Lincoln reached out a hand and stroked Taboo's nose.

"Is that who you were looking for, Fonzy? I didn't even think about..." Her eyes widened, and she drew in a sharp breath. What was it with people not breathing right around me?

"Mrs. Lincoln?"

Her eyes narrowed, and she zapped me with a look that should have scorched my entire being. "Did you find another body? Or did you make it happen this time?" she asked, and I backed up a step, right into Dean. His hand came up under my elbow to steady me, but I shook him off.

"I did not make anything happen. I found poor Emma in her refrigerator at the shop when Taboo here started barking in the back, and I called the police. All I've heard is that she had a heart attack, and no one was there to help her. I didn't want to ask because I could see you were distraught over your missing dog, but now that you have him back, can you please tell me what the jerk on the phone told you again? And elaborate. Don't leave anything out."

She took a second to look down at her dog, and then back up at me. "I'm...sorry."

I held in my gasp. It would have only made her mad if I'd sucked in air like I wanted to. But I didn't think I'd ever heard her apologize before—for anything. This was the woman who would demand that the cops come out and shoot—or at least arrest—the squirrels for trying to eat the bird seed in her feeder. She'd yell at anyone who came to her house, even if you were dropping off a present. She was often cranky and gave a wicked side-eye to all passersby. I wasn't sure why she was like this, or when it started, but it had been as long as I'd been alive that I knew of. And yet she'd just apologized.

I was going to be the bigger person here and simply nodded.

She nodded back. "I had let Fonzy out into the yard after dinner, and he went to the fence to see his best friend, Taboo, who is always home at that time. Rick had left me a message yesterday that they wouldn't be home, so I hadn't expected them and told Fonzy that his friend should be back this evening, since he missed him last night. Emma closes the store to come home and make dinner at her usual time every other day, and our dogs always greet each other at the fence."

I had not realized that Emma and Rick lived behind Mrs. Lincoln. I filed it away in my brain to put on my clue board once I had it set up. And when did Rick call her? But she went on before I could ask.

"When I went out to call Fonzy in, he was not there, and no matter how much I called him, he wouldn't come to me. When I went out into the yard, I found the side yard gate swinging open, and I panicked. I called Shirleen to ask for someone to help me find my poor little boy when a man took the phone from her and said that no one would be out to help me unless I had information about a dead body. They were looking for the person who killed someone, and you were at fault."

"He said I was at fault?" What a jerk!

"Yes, those were the words he used, and then he hung up on me." She tucked the little dog in closer to her chest, and he put his head on her shoulder, still keeping his eye on Taboo. "I already apologized, so I'm not going to do it again, but that wasn't right that he said that. It got my dander up, though, and then I came right over here."

"And you didn't see Fonzy on the porch swing when you came..." I almost said storming up, but quickly changed my words because there would be no value in agitating her. "When you came up to the door? I'm not asking because I think you're neglectful, I promise. I'm just trying to pin down the time. What were we all doing for someone to be able to come up, put your dog on the swing, tie him up, even if it wasn't really tied, and then leave, when the only thing we did was talk for a few moments, and then Dean left to get you a soda?"

She nodded. "I knew that."

I was still glad I said it because it seemed to get her dander to go down. I'd have to keep that in my back pocket for any future interactions.

She kissed Fonzy on his crown. "No, I did not see him, and I guarantee you I would have. If nothing else, he would have barked if he'd seen me. I know where he is at all times. Except tonight."

"You didn't see anyone in the yard? No one waved at you from the sidewalk, or was lurking around when you let Fonzy out?" I asked.

She shook her head. "No, and normally I would have followed him out into the yard because I always do, but—" She cut herself off and bit her lip. "But my phone rang, and I went back into the house, telling Fonzy to go find Taboo and then behave."

Interesting. "And who was on the phone?"

"No one." She stroked the dog's back, then took a seat on the bench so Taboo could come up and rest his head on her lap right next to Fonzy. "When I said hello, there was some background noise like kids yelling, or a radio, and then a click."

"An actual click? Like someone putting the phone down?"

"That's what I said, didn't I?" Dander rising alert.

"Yes, yes, you did, it's just that if the person had been on a cell phone, there wouldn't have been a click, so I was trying to make sure that the noise was there because that would mean it had to be a landline." Or a phone booth, but there was only one of those in town, and it happened to reside in my house.

She clamped her lips shut and looked off into the distance. "There was definitely a click, and what sounded like a TV on in the background. It was definitely a landline."

"Did it come up as a number on your phone?"

"It might have? Let me check." Without a word, she handed Fonzy over to me so she could reach into her purse for her phone.

I did my best to foist the dog off on Dean, but my new husband was not paying attention. Fonzy and I stared at each other, each on the defensive, wondering if the other would bite. Well, I was wondering that. He was probably wondering what bite to do first. He bared his teeth just as Mrs. Lincoln gasped. "The call came from Emma's house."

"Emma's house?" Dean asked, finally getting in on the conversation. To be fair, I hadn't given him much of a chance to talk, but I appreciated it now.

I would have asked the same thing, but I was still watching Fonzy to make certain he was pausing on his desire to take a chunk out of my arm or face. Taboo came up at that moment and leaned into my leg. I put a hand down to stroke his head, and Fonzy rumbled low in his chest. Taboo leaned harder, so I scratched his head. Poor Moose was going to have a fit that I smelled so much like a dog when this was over.

"Yes, this is the number for the phone they have in the house in case someone needs to call them from their family."

"But there was no one at Emma's house," Dean answered. "Rick is in the hospital, and Emma is gone. Is there anyone else living there that you know of?"

Good question. I waited to see if Mrs. Lincoln would, or could, answer.

"I have no idea. I don't interfere in other people's lives."

Just those of the local wildlife if they were doing things she found distasteful, like eating birdseed that wasn't meant for them. Got it.

"I'm sorry, Mrs. Lincoln, I wasn't insinuating that you interfered in anything. I was simply asking because you see them and their dog. I wasn't sure if they'd mentioned someone staying with them."

She harrumphed. Because, of course, she did.

Dean let it go and continued. "So, we have a call from a house where presumably no one was there, about a dog that was either taken, or deliberately let out of the gate, since I know for certain Mrs. Lincoln would not leave that gate unlatched when letting the dog out."

Oh, nothing like a little dig. Though it couldn't have happened that way because someone had taken the dog and then brought him here and tied him on the porch swing. Unless he had escaped and someone had found him, who knew that Mrs. Lincoln was here, and didn't want to get involved with the curmudgeonly lady. So, they decided to tie him up to the swing instead of handing him over to her personally. I wouldn't have blamed them, but that seemed pretty extreme.

Okay, then, back to who would have taken the dog, another mystery I didn't need.

"Well, it doesn't matter at this point," Mrs. Lincoln said, taking Fonzy from me. "I have my dog back, and I'm going home. You all can do your sleuthing, or whatever you call it, since it's really nothing more than sticking your nose in where it isn't needed. I'll go back to keeping to myself and not letting this little darling out of my sight."

"Don't you want to know who took Fonzy, though?" I asked. "What if they do it again?"

"They won't." She held the little dog tighter as Taboo continued leaning against my leg.

"But they could, and don't you find it odd that someone called you just as you put Fonzy out, and the call came from a house that would have been empty at the time, and the person said nothing, just hung up on you?" My brain would be on fire with needing to know who, what, when, why, and how. Heck, my brain was on fire for those very answers, and the dog wasn't even mine.

"I'll leave that to you. I don't know anything more than what I told you. There is no way this dog is ever leaving my side again. Let me know when you find out, and then I can press charges for dognapping. I'll get my case together to slam dunk them. No one messes with my poochie."

Poochie? I didn't ask because Mrs. Lincoln turned and left the porch, heading back down the stairs to then hit the sidewalk and make the short journey home to her house that fronted the river.

"We'll walk you home," Poobah said, clicking his tongue for Taboo to join them.

"Well, that was weird and yet interesting," Dean said, tucking my hand into his.

"Is it something we should put on the board? You know, whenever we actually get it set up?"

He squeezed my fingers, then brought our hands up to kiss my knuckles. "I think it's definitely something we at least want to keep in mind. Who was playing games with Mrs. Lincoln, and why, when the house should have been empty? And why on the landline? It's all very strange."

"When isn't stuff strange around here? I think I'd be looking for the other shoe to drop if something actually worked just as it was supposed to on any given day." I turned into his embrace and lay my cheek against his chest. He rested his chin on the top of my head, and he laughed, but the sound abruptly cut off, just as his grip tightened. Footsteps sounded behind me, climbing the stairs to the porch. Who was it this time?

He drew in a quick breath. "I'm surprised to see you here, and on a night like this. How did you get here? Does Caper know you were coming?"

"Can I come in first, Dean? Or are you going by a new name now? I never could keep those things straight."

I turned to find a blonde woman with a bag in one hand and a jacket in the other. Her whole demeanor was a picture of defeat, and yet, her words were full of sarcasm.

"It's Dean, it's always been Dean."

"Right." She laughed in an incredibly caustic way. "Just the last name got kicked around. Hey, I got kicked around for the last name, too, but I couldn't hide it. You're luckier than me." That laugh and snark turned into quivering lips and wrapping her arms around herself as she plopped down on the very swing where we'd found Fonzy.

What on earth was going on? Who was this? I had no idea about the first one, but the things she had said clicked in my head. I had a feeling I knew who was standing before us. If I was right, things were very possibly about to get extremely complicated, and I couldn't stop it.

Chapter 13

I looked over the woman's features, making her younger in my mind, and melding her with Caper, and I came up with a combination that made me draw in a sharp breath.

"You must be the infamous Roxy," the woman said, after righting herself and sweeping her light hair away from her face. "Amelia has nothing but complete adoration for you. I would be happy with even ten percent of that kind of admiration," she said.

Was this Amelia and Isaac's mother? Oh, wow.

Part of me wanted to glance over at Dean to see how he was handling this, but I didn't want to look away from the woman sitting in front of me, appearing equal parts defeated and aggressively raring for a fight.

Yet, I didn't want the silence to go on for too long, so I jumped in. "I'm Roxy. We haven't met before. Why don't you come in? I can put some tea on, if that suits you?" As I stepped back, I had to use my elbow to get Dean to move out of the way. I shot a look at him with my eyebrows furrowed and my lips in a flat line. I knew a lot about the parts of the family who lived here on the property, but I didn't know everything about the family situation outside of that. No one ever talked about the kids' mom to me. But if we were actually going to deal with this, it was not going to be out on the porch with the poor woman standing in the doorway.

Dean finally stepped back. His shoulders were stiff, and his phone was already in his hand. "You two can have your tea. I'm going to go talk with Caper." And with that, he walked toward the dining room, most likely heading out to the house in the back where Caper, Amelia, and Isaac were probably sleeping.

Which meant that this woman and I were left staring at each other.

"I'm sorry," she said. "I shouldn't have come without letting anyone know. I didn't have anywhere else to go, though, and I was hoping to at least talk to Caper before I figured out where I'd be heading next."

"Come on in. I'm sorry, I don't remember your name." I realized that at the last second and just asked instead of prancing around it until it got awkward.

"Willow Winchester." She held her bag in front of her chest like it was some kind of shield. I had no intention of attacking her, but I wasn't going to tell her that because I didn't know what kind of person she was. Yet.

Opening the door wider, I waited for her to come in. Still, she hesitated. So, I reached out to grab her arm, pulling her into the foyer, and closing the door behind her. I might not know her, but I was going to act the way I would with anyone else. If only I were able to read auras, like my cousin. But since I couldn't, I was going to have to go with my gut, which rarely failed me.

"Do you like tea?" I asked, leading the way into the kitchen. We could sit at the island so that we weren't staring at each other. Also, we could start talking while I prepared the tea, which meant she could talk without me looking at her.

"Yes. I haven't had it in a while, so a cup of English breakfast would be great, if you don't mind. Since it's so late, we're probably not supposed to drink it now, but it would be nice."

"We're not snobby tea people here. You can have whatever you want whenever you want it."

When I glanced at her, she smiled. It was a sad smile, and I could see, out of my peripheral vision, that it fell away as soon as I looked back at my task. I kept my eyes on the electric tea kettle while I filled it up, pushed the button to get it rolling, and then pulled two mugs from the cabinet above my head. I'd have the breakfast tea, too, just to prove that we weren't exactly an establishment of rules around here. Reference the fact that Caper had not always been the paragon of parenthood that he was now, and Dean's previous slate wasn't exactly clean, either. Not to mention, I had a whole other facet of my life that few knew about.

"Cream? Sugar?" I asked, opening the wooden tea box and pulling out two sachets.

"Both? If you don't mind?"

"Not at all. Do you want to do it yourself?" I rearranged some of the teas in their little wooden cubbies to avoid looking at her.

"You can just make it like you would make it for yourself. I don't actually know much about tea." And there was that exhaustion creeping back into her voice. "Look, Roxy, I understand you're probably the hostess with the mostest, and I saw the sign out in the front yard that the wedding to Dean was today. I don't want to rain on your beautiful parade, but I didn't want Caper to ignore my call, and I just wanted to check in with him. I don't need to stay, and you certainly don't need to make me tea or even try to make me comfortable. I know what everyone thinks of me, and I don't expect any less disdain than I get."

Because of where I was standing, I was able to catch a glimpse of Dean and Caper walking across the yard. My new husband looked up, right at me, and I shook my head. Fortunately, Dean got my signal, and Willow missed it altogether. I needed more time.

There was a cookbook right in front of me on display. My talent allowed me to use anything that was a book. I didn't often try to change the ingredients list in a cookbook into an answer for a question I was going to secretly ask, but these times seemed to call for stepping outside my box. Who was I kidding? The box had been destroyed the first time I'd found a dead body and had only expanded from there.

"Actually, if you're open to it, I could make London Fog. Are you okay with Earl Grey tea?" Still not looking at her, I grabbed the cookbook from the bookshelf, as if I'd need it to help me.

"Sure."

I imagined her shrugging her shoulders and moving her light hair off her face again, as I silently asked my question of what the right way was to handle this, and then flipped the book open to the middle.

The letters immediately sparkled and rose from the pages of some cookbook from the early nineteen hundreds. The gold flecks held in the air for a moment and then swirled above the page, forming letters.

There was an audible gasp behind me, and it startled me so badly that I flipped the book closed without waiting to see what words were being formed. Whipping around, I found Willow with her hand over her mouth, and her blue eyes opened so wide I was afraid she was about to faint.

Had she seen the sparkles? We'd thought that the talent had passed down to Amelia through her mom's side of the family, but this was proof positive, and I wasn't sure I was ready for that. Maybe I shouldn't have silently told Dean and Caper not to come in.

Willow and I stared at each other for what felt like an eternity. I wasn't sure who was going to be the first one to speak, but I really didn't want it to be me.

"I wasn't sure if we'd see you," Caper said behind me. His voice was quiet, and there was a yearning that made me wonder about their relationship. I'd often wondered if he kept in contact with her while she was in jail. Had he thought he had to talk with her, or was it because he couldn't take the way things had fallen apart between them over the years?

Her sigh hinted she was going to be sarcastic in her response, but then she looked up at him, back at me, then at Dean, and buried her face in her hands.

"This is too much." Her words were mumbled by her hands, but I could still hear her crying and see the way her shoulders shook with every ragged breath. "I should never have come here. You were done with me, and I should have let that stand. I'm sorry." She rose from her perch at the island. Grabbing her backpack, she shot out of the kitchen.

Dean, Caper, and I all shared a look, not sure who was going to go after her, but I was certain it couldn't be all of us.

And then it was none of us because, as the door to the kitchen swung closed, I saw Amelia waiting for her mom in the lobby.

I put my arm out to stop the two men from leaving the kitchen, just for a moment.

"Willow saw the sparkles when I asked the cookbook a question. She looked like she'd seen a ghost, but Earl doesn't seem to be around, so I'm going to assume that she is fully capable of seeing and using the talent. Has she ever done that around you, Caper?"

"No, not that I know of, but then I can't say we did much, but fight about things and make mistakes left and right between us, so I'm not sure she would have told me regardless."

"She's never done anything around me," Dean said.

"And around the kids?" I asked, trying to get a bead on what we might be working with here. Had she given up her talents to be with Caper, and now that she thought she had nothing to come home to they were resurging? To be honest, I had no idea how it all worked. The only people I knew had not given up their talents and had instead found someone they could live with and still be everything they were. I'd have to look into the family books and messages Poobah had put together to see if there was any record of that.

But not right now. Because right now, I could hear Amelia talking in low tones, but I wasn't able to hear the actual words. Enough time had passed, though, that we should all go out and see what we needed to address and how to do it. I had been okay with a few minutes for Amelia to say what she needed to say, but I didn't want to leave her dealing with this alone if she needed backup or people standing with her, especially since we were right on the other side of the door.

I went out first and found Amelia sitting with her mom on a love seat in the foyer. She was holding her mom's hands. Her smile when she looked up at us emerging from the kitchen was like its own little sun.

"My mom's here!" she said with so much light that it danced around her head, and a small wind kicked up near the front desk. "But you already know that because she couldn't have gotten in without you opening the door." She bit her lip. "Yeah, that makes more sense." And then she laughed and leaned forward to hug Willow.

Willow, who looked like she'd been hit by a stiff breeze on a day where there hadn't been any wind. What was going through her mind?

"Can she stay, Dad? Roxy? I know things are supposed to be quiet around here for the week now that the wedding is over, but I'll give up my bedroom if I have to. I actually like the couch out in the living room."

"Amelia..." Willow said.

"Dean and I just moved onto the third floor," I started, but didn't get to finish because Caper cut me off.

"Look, Roxy is letting us stay in the small cottage out back." Caper hesitated. Because he didn't want her in the house, or because he wanted her there too much? "We'd like you to stay with us."

I was going to offer my old rooms, but if Caper wanted her at the cottage, I wasn't going to jump in and thwart him. Ultimately, it would be up to her.

Willow glanced over at Caper. To see what he thought of the arrangement? I didn't have a book, so I couldn't ask, but I could go with my gut again. And that gut was saying he wanted her to stay, and if it had just been him, he would have done whatever he could to make her stay.

"I would appreciate that," Willow finally said, and it was as if the whole house released the breath we'd all been holding.

Of course, this set up a whole new set of obstacles and things to manage when I had the murder to also take on, but what was one more thing on my plate?

"It's late," I said into the silence. "I'll text Glennis to set up breakfast for everyone tomorrow morning. You'll have time to settle in, and then we can introduce you to my family."

I had no idea if that was a good idea on the whole, but it was the best one I could think of. And if it meant that croissants were lobbed across the table and words along with them, then we'd handle that when it happened. Right now, it was late, I was tired, I had never gotten carried over the threshold, and I was losing steam. Time to go to bed.

But first, Caper asked to get Isaac so that he wouldn't be surprised in the morning. Not to mention, he would probably want to be included, even if it interrupted his beauty sleep. Amelia went with him, singing about how she was going to jump scare her brother. Which left Willow with us again. Isaac was probably snoring away in his own bed, lucky guy. But tomorrow would bring some new things to light, I had a feeling, and I really wished I had caught what the words were from the cookbook before I slammed it shut. Maybe I'd try again before we went up to bed.

Willow was quiet as I showed her around the bottom floor and pointed out all the things she might need. Dean had gone back into the kitchen to finish the tea I had never made.

When he came back, he also had a slice of chocolate cake with peanut butter icing, one of Glennis's most loved desserts.

"Thank you," Willow said. She placed the cake and the tea on the end table next to the couch and then wrung her hands together. "I'm sorry, Dean. I'm sorry I did this. I should have just called."

Dean shook his head and crossed his arms over his chest. "You know what, Willow? I think you're wrong. I think this is exactly what you should have done. Family does stick together, but we need to know what you plan on doing going forward. Caper has made it a point to be here for the kids, and I'm not letting him backslide this time. If you have any intention of staying for any length of time, I'd encourage you to figure out what you're willing to give and give up." He went into the dining room, probably to watch for Caper and the kids to return and give me a minute with the woman.

"He's not mad," I said.

"He wouldn't be wrong if he were mad, Roxy." She sat down on the couch and pulled the cake toward her. "I haven't done the right thing often, if we're being honest with each other here, but I felt drawn to this place when they opened the door to my cage. Now, I feel that there's something I'm supposed to be doing here, but I don't know what it is."

Was she going to bring up the magic she'd witnessed in the kitchen? Did she know Amelia had talent also?

Glancing at the clock on the wall, I realized it was getting late, and I was exhausted.

"We'll talk more in the morning." I looked her over. "Please don't leave without telling anyone. I understand there's a lot going on, and I get it if you feel overwhelmed, but Amelia shouldn't have to wonder where you are, or why you left after she just got to see you again."

"You're even better at that than Dean and Caper combined. Interesting."

"Better at what?"

"The 'listen to me and follow what I say because I'm making sense,' but really you're telling me what to do, while also trying to shame me."

I literally took a step back. "That is not something I would ever do, and I'm sorry that's your first thought when I was simply trying to look out for a child whom I love and ask you to help me help her. I wasn't saying you couldn't leave, just that you let her know before you do. Caper should be back any minute now, if he can get Isaac to wake up. I'll let you get settled. You can leave your cake plate and cup out here when you're done. I'll have the staff pick it up in the morning. Let me know if you need anything else." And I turned to leave without looking at her again.

"I'm sorry," she said with a hitch in her voice that could only be tears on the very verge of spilling over again.

I was not stupid. I had dealt with a lot of people over the years, both as family and guests. She was hurting and probably scared, and I did understand to some extent, but I didn't have to be her punching bag. She would do whatever she was going to do.

However, I wouldn't give up the opportunity to say what I had to say and then later regret that I hadn't said something if she chose to leave in the middle of the night.

"I am in so many different places in my head right now, and being back out in society hasn't always been my forte. And that sparkle thing you did in the kitchen threw me off my already rocky horse and right into the mud of anxiety, mixed with the ashes of what I thought was my marriage. It's not an excuse, I promise, but there's just a lot here that I wasn't expecting."

I did finally turn back around and gave her my full attention, but I didn't say anything yet.

She had paused, but she hadn't asked me any questions, and I wasn't answering with more information than she needed, or would understand, until I knew more about her.

"Tough customer." There was the sarcasm again. I had expected it, so it didn't take me off guard this time. "My dad used to be able to do little tricks with candles, making the flames have the hiccups and dance at his command. He even made it giggle once, and it was the best memory I have of growing up."

"Your dad?" I asked. I wasn't going to sit just yet, and I'd let her lead the conversation, but I wasn't missing the opportunity to get more information, if she was willing to share it.

"My dad, yeah." Her eyes glassed over again, but she didn't let any of the tears spill. "I wasn't allowed to tell my mom he could do stuff like that. He made me keep it a total secret after she saw it one day and had a total fit, full-on screaming and yelling. The people next door even came over to see what was wrong, and she lied, but we never talked about it again. Yet, every once in a while, my dad would make a candle flicker and dance, and it felt warm in my heart in a way I've never felt again. But I wish I could." She hadn't been looking at me during her whole speech, but now she flicked her glance up to mine and seemed to be searching for something.

Because I wasn't sure what it could be, I let her look her fill and kept myself in one place. I was not going to give her any answers until I had a better handle on how much she knew and what pieces she didn't have.

"What were the sparkles? Are you like a witch?"

"Not a witch, she's a mancer," Amelia said, skipping into the room. "And so am I!"

Well, then, Plan B, or was it Plan G now? I'd lost count.

Chapter 14

"Does your dad know you're here?" Willow asked Amelia when the young girl settled on the couch next to her.

"He knows if I'm not in the house that I'm here."

Willow quirked an eyebrow at her daughter, and I did my best to hide a smile. Different parenting might be on the horizon, and I was not against that at all.

"So, you didn't tell him you were leaving the house?"

Amelia bit her lip and shook her head. "I guess it would be nicer if I told him instead of making him wonder, wouldn't it?"

"It would. Your dad has a lot of things going on. Worrying about where you are doesn't have to be one of them."

Talk about a master. Willow pulled her daughter into her side and gave her a hug to add a positive aspect to what she was asking instead of making it a guilt thing. I highly approved, not that anyone was asking me.

"Is he still trying to get Isaac to wake up?" I moved to stand in front of the two females snuggled up on the couch in the foyer.

"Blech, not wake up, but to get himself together. He was totally disoriented, and then he started running around the house and cleaning up things. He won't come over until the whole place is shiny and clean, and then he wants to take a shower before coming over."

Willow smiled. "It's not a bad thing to want to feel proud of how you look and probably smell. Am I right?"

"You are." Amelia crept even closer to her mother, even though I wouldn't have thought that was possible, since they were pretty much melded together, yet somehow she managed it.

"How long do you think they're going to be?" I asked, not wanting to leave before they got here, but also knowing that it was my wedding night and I would like to be upstairs with my new husband.

"I don't know, but I was going to go in the phone booth if it took them too long. I've been having fun with triple digits. You should try the nines. I can stay here, though, with my mom instead."

"You can go if you need to, Roxy. We'll get settled, and then we'll see you in the morning, like you said. Breakfast is soon enough, I think, and it might be good if it's just the four of us when we're all together for the first time in a while." Willow's face took on a hopeful, almost wistful look, and it gave me hope.

She was not wrong, and I didn't feel dismissed, so much as given a pass to leave if I chose to. I liked this woman a whole lot and hoped she would be able to get over some of her rougher aspects. Make a commitment to living a life that was not only good for her but also for her children, who obviously loved her and wanted her to be here.

"It's probably going to be a little bit, honestly," Amelia said. "The house is not exactly as clean as it should be, and Dad knows it, which is why he's helping Isaac instead of prodding him along to come right over. You know how those guys are."

I did, and so I said good night, trusting my gut that this was the better way for it to be. I texted Dean to let him know I was heading upstairs. We didn't need to be here. They were all safe, and a meeting with just the little family, without any interlopers, did make the most sense.

I took that thought with me as I climbed the two sets of stairs to the third floor. It totally felt like a slog after everything that had happened today. Maybe I would look more fully into installing an elevator. I had no idea where I'd put it, of course, but it kept my mind off what was going on downstairs, and let me think about something else. I should have been celebrating my wedding night, and I would, but maybe not for the next flight of stairs.

When I got to the top of all the stairs, it was to find the door open, and a trail of even more rose petals than I had laid down hours ago, leading farther into the apartment that was flooded with soft candlelight.

"Too much light?" Dean asked, coming out of the galley kitchen with a steaming mug in each hand. "Hot chocolate, extra marshmallows, Mrs. Winchester. Just what the groom ordered. Or I would have ordered, if it had been earlier, and Glennis had still been here. But since she isn't, you'll have to settle for my version, which involved ripping open packets of hot chocolate mix and dumping in the hot water." He handed over the mug. "I would like points for extra marshmallows, though."

"You totally get all the extra points," I said.

He set the mugs on the coffee table we'd gotten out of the storage in the basement. I thought he'd hand me one, but instead he shooed me away with flapping hands. "Go get your pajamas on. I know we're going to have a lot to talk about, and I guarantee you I have a lot to say. So, let's be comfortable saying it. Extra bonus, I know how much you like your marshmallows to melt in the hot chocolate before you drink it. It'll be the perfect temperature when you get back, Goldilocks."

Not much I could do except follow his directive, especially when that was what I wanted more than anything else right now. My shoes were cute, but even cute shoes could be uncomfortable after walking in them for hours and hours. And we did have a lot to talk about, which would be better done in stretchy pants.

I only hoped I had enough strength to ask the hard questions.

"Let me start, if you don't mind." Dean was sitting on the couch when I came back out of our bedroom. He patted the cushion next to him and then grabbed my mug to hand it to me as I sat down.

"Okay." Since I had no idea where to start, or even what to ask, I was more than willing to be led through this one. Surely, I'd have questions, but they'd be better questions if I let him go first.

"There's a lot of history with Caper's family, and some of it is particularly rocky."

"I figured as much."

"The thing is that I don't know very much about it myself. Caper would rarely, if ever, talk to me about anything having to do with Willow. That's her real name, from what I remember, though, the last time I saw her, she was going by Lisa. He never answered my questions, never confided in me, and when I left them all behind to start again, he wouldn't tell me what happened to get her in jail in the first place."

"I suppose there are records we could look into." I took a sip of my absolutely amazing cocoa and smiled at him.

Cupping my face with one of his huge hands, he leaned in to kiss that smile. When he pulled back, he sighed. "I promised myself I would never do that. Caper has a right to his privacy, as long as it never hurts his kids, and the reason for her incarceration is really not my business. I hope you understand."

"I do, and we'll leave it alone then. I don't want to make more trouble for them. As long as she stays on the straight and narrow while she's here, I have no need to know what she's doing or what she did before. We all have secrets." Although the mancer one was out of the bag with Willow.

"We do, and some we'd like to keep."

I nodded while I took another sip. Honestly, best cocoa ever, though I certainly wouldn't be telling that to Glennis, or she'd never make me her special kind again. It involved Irish cream, and she did wonders with the stuff.

"So, what is our plan?" I asked. "Do we just let things unfold as they will for them down in the cottage, and focus on the murder of Emma? I'm actually very nervous about the new chief. What if he manufactures evidence? He seems completely bent on making me the culprit, and I know, without a shadow of a doubt, I did nothing. But he doesn't seem to care about the facts."

"He's delusional, but it is concerning that he shut off the cameras and threatened you. Do you at least feel safe on the whole?" Dean asked.

"I'll feel safer if I pretty much just stay here and be the collector of information, instead of the one out and about trying to collect it, as I have before."

He nodded. "I'm on board with that. We'll play it by ear, and only step into things that we absolutely cannot stay out of. You have a good team here, both for running an inn and for protecting the family circle you've built."

"You're just saying that because you want to get lucky tonight," I said, then laughed when he took my hot chocolate mug out of my hands.

He kissed my knuckles and said, "Is it working?"

"Yes, dear husband of mine, it is."

***

Thankfully, I had remembered to text Glennis last night as I'd climbed all of those stairs, so breakfast smells were wafting up to the third floor when I emerged from our rooms and started the descent with Dean right behind me.

"We're going to take this one thing at a time," I said. "No need to tackle everything at once."

"Do you really think that's going to happen?" Dean said with a chuckle.

"No, but maybe if I say it out loud, I can manifest it. Clean-cut things would be nice."

He placed a hand on my shoulder, stopping me on the stairs, and then gently turning me around. "I'm not going to deny it would be nice, but I think we both need to remember this is a family of chaos. If we set our expectations lower, then we could be pleasantly surprised, instead of trying to rein things in."

"That makes too much sense, Dean."

That got an actual laugh. "I'm not saying I'll be able to do it, just that we might want to at least try."

"I can do that. Great job on Day One of being a husband."

"Isn't this technically Day Two?"

"Don't lose your points before you even get to count them."

"So noted."

I reached up on my tiptoes to give him a kiss, then turned back around and walked down the rest of the stairs.

I could hear the cacophony before I even reached the dining room doors. So many people were talking and also laughing. That, at least, was a good sign. After I'd texted Glennis, I'd also texted my family in a group chat to let them know the basics without taking up too much time or space. I'd wanted to get up to Dean and didn't want to field too many questions I didn't have answers for. But at least my sisters and brother-in-law, along with my parents, had been prepared. I heard a particular guffaw and realized that Uncle Vince was here, which probably meant Aunt Hellen was here, too. I couldn't imagine that they had left Poobah without a quick text to have him come over, too.

Chaos was bound to erupt. I did hope someone had warned Willow about not talking about our talents or magic in the common areas. The staff would be able to see anything that was done on the television in the kitchen, even if they couldn't hear it.

Caper nodded at me as soon as we cleared the doors, and I figured he had meant that as he had taken care of things. Willow looked a little overwhelmed, but she'd get used to it when she stayed. Or that could be "if," but I was going with optimism this time and would stick to that unless someone proved me wrong.

There were two seats open at the top of the table. I took the one next to Mena, and Dean sat next to his brother. I wasn't sure if it had been planned for the two families to sit across from each other, but I liked it. It gave all of my family the opportunity to look at all of Dean's family, and there were so many smiles, my heart was about to burst.

But first, my mouth was watering because Glennis had put on quite the spread. The recipe that had caused so many issues a year ago was very proudly laid out in the middle of a smorgasbord of what I would swear was probably every breakfast item that anyone had enjoyed eating in the last century.

There was a chorus of hellos when we stood behind our seats and grabbed our plates. Everyone else had already taken a turn through the line, from what I could tell.

"Oh! Monkey bread," I sighed and dug right in. I listened to the chatter resume behind me. A lot of it was recommendations for what things Willow might want to see around town, and where she could go to do some actual decorating, since Caper wasn't exactly all about making it a home. Isaac playfully defended his father, and Amelia groaned.

It was like any other family dinner I had ever been to, and yet there was a slight underpinning of no one being entirely sure of what they were allowed to say, what they should, or should not know, or what was off-limits.

We'd have to break that and just be honest about where we were and who we were, and hope that being that kind of transparent together would make everyone feel more comfortable in general.

Taboo sat to Poobah's left with his head on his lap, while staring longingly up at him as he ate sausage. I watched Poobah slip him a piece off his fork. When the old man looked up at me, he just smiled.

But seeing the dog made me think more about what we were all doing here, and how many different offshoots of things were going on there. I couldn't get over the idea that they all had to be a part of one big body of things, but I had no idea what that body looked like.

And was Willow a part of it? If so, how?

With my plate full, I took my seat again and started digging into the delicious food. Glennis had totally outdone herself, and I so appreciated her. Everything was awesome.

The cinnamon rolls were so wonderfully sweet, too, until Norm opened the door with a fierce expression on his face, and suddenly they turned bitter in my mouth.

What now?

Chapter 15

"What now?" And yes, I did say that out loud after I'd already said it in my head. I probably could have been nicer, but he could have waited until after I'd eaten my fill before bothering me.

Micah came into the room behind him and sent a little wave to Mena, who returned it while also puckering her lips. Well, at least they'd made up to a certain extent. One less thing to worry about, though, if I had been given a choice, I would have kept that one and given up the murder case. But I hadn't been allowed to see what was behind door two.

Norm cleared his throat when he saw that everyone was in the dining room, eating, and he had not been invited.

"Sorry, sorry, I would say I could come back at a later time, but I can't, so I won't." He fiddled with the brim on his hat and then took it off to crush it at his waist. What on earth was making him so nervous, and how did I get him to go away without telling me so I could go back to eating my lovely monkey bread in peace?

"Just spit it out, Norm. Whatever you have to say can be said here."

"The chief has some evidence he thinks can prove that you poisoned Emma and killed her, then shoved her in the refrigerator in the back and just pretended that the door was locked when I was trying to get in."

"What?" I was getting tired of saying that word and various versions of it, but I had nothing else to go with.

"He said he lifted prints off the locking mechanism. Yours are the only ones on there."

"I opened it for you. Of course, my prints are on there."

"He also said they found poisoned chocolates Emma must have eaten. I had to tell him that you had taken a box with you when you took the flowers. I'm sorry, but I couldn't lie. He found another box and had it tested, and there was definite poison and one missing. The coroner is redoing the autopsy and testing for the poison. Did anyone eat from the box you took with you?"

Norm might not have wanted to lie, but I wasn't against at least skirting around the truth here.

"What poison was it?" I asked instead of answering his question.

"I don't know yet, but the chief wants me to get the chocolates from you to be able to test them. He presumes you only left the box with poison, or if you had poisoned two of them, you took the second one with you when the first did its job, so no one would be able to pin it on you. Sorry."

"Norm, stop apologizing and grab some food," Mom said. "There's still plenty on the sideboard. You, too, Micah. There's something bigger going on here, and I think we're going to need to discuss it all."

My dad pulled up two additional chairs, and everyone scooted around the table so we could make room for the two officers. Micah took the seat right next to Mena, and Norm sat next to him on the other side of Anjanetta.

My older sister gave him his plate and shooed him away to the food table behind her. When his back was turned, we all exchanged some quick looks of "what the hell were we going to do now," while he and Micah chose from the many offerings on the sideboard. They could be there for a little while. Even longer if I made it that way. Using my eyes and a jerk of my head, I sent Mena over to help them make their choices.

I had a couple of options here. Mena had not actually gone to the hospital for the poisoning. She'd been sick, but my mom had fixed her. Unfortunately, I couldn't tell him that, but I also couldn't lie outright to him. For one thing, I didn't have the box to hand over to prove that we didn't touch them.

Crap!

When Mena, Micah, and Norm returned to the table, Norm opened his mouth, and my mom cut him off.

"Micah, were you able to find anything regarding the request I had?"

He had already forked some of Glennis's famous waffles into his mouth. He chewed as fast as he could to answer Diana Gleason, who smiled at him and gestured for him to take his time.

But he didn't. He swallowed quickly and wiped his mouth with a linen napkin Mena handed him from her place setting. "Yes, ma'am, I looked into it, and you're right that there seemed to be something off about her. I wasn't able to dive too deep, as I was pulled away from the investigation to accompany Norm here to the inn."

"Chief has made him my watchdog. I guess we'll see who he's the most loyal to." Norm jammed a piece of toast in his mouth and avoided making eye contact.

"Norm, could it be that Micah is protecting you by being here, and he can confirm anything the two of you come up with together? But if he plays the antagonist when around the chief, then that jerk of a man will believe he really is watching for you to make a mistake. And yet, in reality, he's helping you do the things you need to?" Belmont Gleason, Dad, as I called him, was not someone to mess with when it came to logic.

"It could." Norm turned to his co-worker. "Is that it?"

"I think it would be better if I keep my thoughts on that to myself, so I don't have to lie if asked to confirm or deny."

Norm harrumphed. "Fair enough. Now, what's this investigation you're doing that you got called off of?"

After placing his napkin on the table and giving a wistful look to his unfinished plate of delightful food, Micah launched into what he'd been doing since that first night. "Mena's mom asked if I could look into the deceased because she'd been asking around, and no one seemed to have seen or heard of her until about ten years ago. The earliest thing I could find is a driver's license issued about eleven years ago when she moved here with Rick, her husband. There is literally nothing about her before then. No birth records, no passports, no social media, nothing. I should have brought my folder to show you the searches I did and the lack of what I found when I put in keywords."

"Interesting," Diana said. "And you dug back as far as you could?"

"Yes, ma'am."

"You don't have to call me that, Micah. Diana is fine, especially since I think you and I will be talking more in the near future." She flicked a look over to her youngest daughter. "For a variety of reasons. For now, why don't you come back later with the full information you have? You and Isaac can pool your resources and see if our young investigator can dive into things that you wouldn't be able to find on your system?"

Isaac blushed, and Willow wrapped a hand around his shoulder, then kissed the top of his head.

I hadn't had a chance to ask how things had gone last night at the cottage, but currently Caper was sitting next to Dean, then Isaac sat to his left, Willow was next, and then Amelia. All of them had a kind of glow that I associated with true happiness. I only hoped it would stay.

"While Isaac and Micah are doing things that I'd rather not know about, so I don't have to lie, too, can you please tell me about the chocolates?"

"They did come in the house," Poobah said, dropping a hand to stroke Taboo's head. "But I dumped them down the garbage disposal because they smelled wrong. I can get the box out of the trash can if Glennis hasn't had it emptied, but I'm not going to be able to get you the chocolates themselves. They're long gone."

Norm sighed. "That's better than nothing, I guess. Chief isn't going to be happy, but then he hasn't been happy since he stepped foot in the door, so that's not out of the norm." He gave a half laugh at his own quip.

Poobah joined him, and so did my dad. Good enough.

When Poobah rose from his chair, Taboo was right on his heels, and the elderly man smiled down at the dog, as if he were his best friend. What were we going to do when Rick came back to pick the dog up? I might have to consider looking into getting Poobah his own dog, same breed, hopefully the same temperament.

My grandfather headed to the kitchen, where supposedly the box for the chocolates was in the trash. I had no idea if it actually was, since I hadn't handled that end of things when Mena was so sick last night. But if Poobah said he could get it, then he probably could. Or he could tell Micah it was gone, and that would be the end of that.

Either way, we still had Norm to deal with, Norm, who looked like he was not having his best day, but was still trying to put on a brave face. I'd given him grief before when we'd clashed over any number of things, but I really did feel bad for him this time. That chief was a piece of work, and I couldn't imagine having to work with someone who was that awful.

"Is the chief permanent or just interim?" I asked, forking up a piece of scrapple and dipping it in apple butter.

"I have no idea," Norm answered. "He was completely sprung on us out of nowhere. And I can't seem to get anyone to tell me how long he'll be here, and what his authority is. We call him chief, but I'm not certain that's what he actually is. There seem to be some gaps in his record, but I tried looking into it and got blocked out."

"That is strange." And maybe something we could also put Isaac on. I was certain that Micah had done the best job he could, but Isaac was an absolute whiz at this kind of stuff. He'd been working on taking courses to be a private investigator, and this could be a really good internship after all he'd found last time we'd looked into a mysterious death. The kid was golden. As long as he stayed on the right side of the law.

I'd have to talk to him about that, just in case, once the cops went home.

Poobah emerged from the kitchen, Taboo still glued to his side, and handed over the slightly mangled and not very good-smelling box. It must have been buried under the banana peels Glennis had thrown in there. She used them with wild abandon when making her delightful banana blueberry bread. A bread I really hoped no one else ate so I could have it for breakfast for the next week, at least.

"You're sure that's the box?" Norm pulled a plastic bag out from a pocket in his jacket and opened it up for Poobah to drop the mangled thing into.

"As far as I know, that was the only box of candy that came into the house yesterday, and it says something about being locally grown under the trash."

"Interesting." Micah took the plastic bag from Norm and turned it around and around without opening it. "It looks like the one at the station, and yet there are some differences that wouldn't be there if they came from the same shop. We'll look into it." He sent sad eyes to his breakfast, probably thinking that now that they'd accomplished their mission, they had to leave. He placed his napkin on the table, but Diana stopped him.

"You're not going anywhere. We have things to discuss, and I will not be rushed through this family brunch. Settle in, and don't leave anything uneaten on your plate. If your chief gives you grief over it, send him my way. I'll deal with him."

She smiled as she said the words, but there was steel behind that gaze. It had come across as formidable to me when I was young. It usually meant I could be in trouble for not doing what I was supposed to do. But now, it encouraged me and made me really look at how awesome my mom was. I wanted to grow up to be here, especially when Micah obediently put his napkin back in his lap and dug into his pile of sausage.

Conversation swirled around the table, some about the murder, some about the wedding yesterday, but not much about Emma herself, or the research Micah had done that Isaac was going to join in on. Every time someone brought it up, my mom would change the subject, saying we'd get to that and not to ruin this wonderful family time.

I was willing to go along with her for right now, but I was absolutely fiending to find out what other information she'd asked for and how Isaac might be able to expand on it.

I glanced over at our new guest a few times, and she seemed to be holding her own, but she was also very quiet. She observed instead of joining in. I wondered if it had anything to do with the cops being here, because she had been talking with her whole body before they'd entered the room, celebrating the things Amelia and Isaac, and even Caper, had done. She rarely answered questions directed at her, but would deflect as soon as possible to put the conversation back in the other person's court.

At first, Amelia couldn't seem to take her eyes off her mom, but then she held her hand on the table, and Amelia seemed to be able to open up to bringing the rest of the table into her sphere.

She even got Norm to laugh, and that was quite an accomplishment.

But soon the meal was over, and Micah agreed to come back with his information once he checked in with the chief to turn in his report that Norm had been on his best behavior.

As soon as they left, I dragged, or rather, invited, my mom and Isaac into the rooms I had recently inhabited until I became Mrs. Winchester. Still couldn't believe that had actually happened, and I was all for getting back to just basking in my new role as soon as we figured out who had killed Emma and why.

With everything that had happened over the last twenty-four hours, I hadn't taken the time to set up my murder board or the room, but I would. For now, I just wanted to know what specifically my mom had asked Micah and what Isaac had found. Dean decided to follow us in as well, but everyone else went into the library so Amelia could show her mother our vast hoarding of books.

"Okay, so what do we have, and what do we need?" I asked as soon as the door shut.

"Isaac, do you mind if I take the lead on this one until Micah gets here?"

"Of course, Mrs. Gleason," he said respectfully.

She yanked him into a hug so fast I would have expected him to have whiplash. "I'm going to need you to call me Grandma, or some other version you and Amelia are comfortable with. You're family, darling, let's make that even more official."

He blushed, like actual full-on flaming red blushed. His gaze dropped to the floor, and he did the classic nudging of the carpet with the toe of his shoe. "I've never had a grandparent, so I'm not sure. I'll talk with Amelia, and we can decide together."

She stood on her tippy toes to kiss him on the forehead, then dropped back down on the couch. "I look forward to the fruits of your conference. If you need any ideas, just let me know. The girls called their grandmother Grand Duchess to go with Poobah's odd name, but we don't have to go that far. Maybe Queenie?" She shrugged. "Whatever you want, as long as it's not as formal as Mrs. Gleason."

He typed something into his phone and then took the other end of the couch.

Diana smiled at him before launching into her information. "There was something very wrong with those chocolates. Not poison, as this incompetent chief seems to think it was, but magic, very dark magic, very old and dark magic. Obviously, we can't ask Micah to look into that, but I was hoping for some kind of connection with Emma involving a talent or something. I was not expecting her to be hidden from the public until only ten years ago. That's fascinating. Isaac, do you think you can dig into that more?"

"Of course, Roxy's Mom." He smiled at his cheekiness. "I have a feeling Amelia's going to weigh in heavily on this name thing because a couple of times I've seen a search engine up with looking at nicknames for grandparents." He clamped his mouth closed as soon as he said it, as if he had talked out of turn, and told secrets he shouldn't have.

"What are the ones she keeps going back to?" I asked.

He sheepishly pulled out his laptop and opened it on the coffee table. After a few keystrokes that went by so fast it felt like a blur, he turned the computer around so that my mom and I could see it.

"Didi and Boppie," Mom read out loud. "I adore them. However, when you talk to her about the names, can you encourage her to change Boppie to Bopper? Belmont was a big music buff back in the day, and I used to tell him he had to stop bopping around the kitchen to whatever he happened to be listening to because he was giving me motion sickness. Bopper perfectly encapsulates him, if she'll go for it."

"She will. I can be persuasive, too, even though that doesn't appear to be my talent." His smile fell a little. "Actually, I don't know if I have one at all, but that's okay."

"Isaac, we don't know that yet. Everyone develops at a different rate, and it could be possible it's just not your time yet," I said.

It warmed my heart when Mom brushed a hand over the back of his head. "Even if it skips you, there are so many other wonderful things you can and will do."

He ducked a little, not to get away from her, but because he appeared to like it too much. I'd seen him do the same thing when I had complimented him, and he didn't know what to do with it.

There were so many possibilities for this relationship, and I desperately hoped that nothing would happen to ruin it or make it go awry. And we could all get back to making the best of what we had once we figured out who had killed Emma, and why the chief of police was so committed to it being me.

Chapter 16

"Now remember, when Micah gets here, we have to keep to only the information we know from the regular avenues. Let him do most of the talking." Isaac, Caper, and Mena had joined me in the dining room.

Willow had chosen to spend some more time with Amelia, who had decided she needed to get her hair cut and have both of them get a pedicure and manicure. I'd called Chessie ahead of time to give her the full-on "go for whatever they wanted," and also add whatever extras they might ask for. I'd accompanied it with the credit card and put it on the inn. My inn, my call. I'd deal with the tax people next year if I had to.

"I'm sure he knows what to do, Roxy," Caper said.

"No, Dad, I appreciate the reminder. It's never a bad thing to make sure we're all on the same page. This is a team thing, and everyone has to have their part. Roxy's part just happens to be the erudite hottie. Or at least that's what Dean calls her."

We all burst out laughing, but I knew who was going to pay a price later tonight for his insolence in that kind of nickname, and his name started with a D. When I heard him groan in the next room, I knew that he knew it, too.

And then there was that cagey smile again on Isaac's face, and I leaned over to give him a hug. "You're lucky you're cute, but Dean's not going to be as lucky..."

"He's lucky enough," Isaac said, squeezing me back before disengaging and stiffening up. "Micah's here."

I hadn't seen or heard anything, but sure enough, the man showed up a second later and was ushered into the room by Aunt Hellen. I glanced over at Caper, and he only had eyes for his boy. Clairvoyance? It would explain a lot and certainly help in his pursuit of being a private investigator, if true. But I'd have to put the idea on the back burner. That back burner was getting overloaded with all the things I had back there.

It was unavoidable, though, because we had a guest. Someone I very much hoped would have some more answers, or at least a direction to go with finding out who had killed Emma and was trying to make it look like I had done the dastardly deed.

Speaking of only having eyes for someone else, it was like Micah was caught in the tractor beam of Mena's gaze. From my vantage point, I watched in fascination as neither of them looked away. I almost called out a few times, because it looked like he was going to trip on his way to her end of the table. Surprisingly enough, he navigated it without issue, despite never looking where he was going. He was only looking at her.

That could work in our favor, or to our detriment, depending on whether Mena was going to behave. Hopefully, she would, due to the seriousness of what he was here for. If they had things to sort out about their on-again, off-again relationship, then they could also put that on the back burner and return to it once we figured out who the murderer really was.

"Thank you so much for coming by, Micah."

His head turned my way, but his gaze stayed focused on my sister. This was going to take a minute, then.

"I have rooms upstairs if you need a moment to stare longingly into each other's eyes for an extended period of time before we talk about the very important issue of a murder in town. *Another* murder, to be precise."

Isaac snickered, and Caper sighed.

Micah visibly shook off the enchantment of staring at Mena. I really hoped she wasn't doing that purposely with her talent to manipulate. She shrugged her shoulders and raised her hands. We'd talk later. That list of people to gab with was growing.

Clearing his throat, Micah took a folder out from under his elbow and placed it on the table as he took a chair across from me. It was a few seats down from Mena and not facing her. That was probably the best we were going to be able to hope for to keep things on track.

He did glance at Mena one more time with a small half-smile. Then he flipped his folder open and folded his hands on top of it, leaning forward with such intent I had to fight against the need to slink back into my chair.

Caper mirrored his posture, though, and thumped his fist on the embroidered tablecloth Glennis had put on after breakfast this morning. She changed it with each meal, and this was actually one of my favorites with its softly aged linen and extensive embroidery. At least if things got testy, there was no food anyone could throw. It had happened before, so it wasn't out of place for me to be concerned.

"Tell us what you found," Caper said. "Your demeanor tells me it's something, or you wouldn't be here."

Good call, and it was nice to have someone else to push Micah. I knew Mena wouldn't be the one to do it, and since I was the one they were trying to pin it on, anything I said could come out as defensive.

"Interestingly enough, as I said before, there is nothing to Emma's history before the last ten years. I have no socials, no addresses, no previous contacts, no idea where she went to school for any of her life, and no marriage license. Nothing. I'm wondering how she got a loan for the shop without any history, so I put a call into the bank manager. Since it's the weekend, I don't expect to hear back from them until at least Monday."

"Nothing?" Isaac said, his fingers running sleekly over his laptop keyboard.

"Nothing. But if you can find something we haven't, then please click clack away. This is really weird, actually. Everyone has some kind of trail on the internet, even if they don't have social accounts. She does have a website and a couple of accounts across the different platforms to sell her flowers and services, but no personal pictures, no identifying information, and there is not a single picture of her anywhere."

"That is bizarre," Mena said, getting up from her chair to move behind Micah. Of course, she had to put her hand on his shoulder to lean over and look at what he had in that folder.

Of course, she did.

But I wasn't going to say anything if it got us any information he hadn't said out loud.

"It's not impossible." Caper got up from his chair, too. He didn't go over to Micah, though. Instead, he paced from one end of the dining room to the other. I tracked him for the first few rounds. And then couldn't do it anymore, because he was giving me motion sickness.

"At her age, though?" Micah asked, with a small tremor in his voice.

Glancing up, I caught the brief smile on my sister's face and just shook my head.

"Yeah, at her age," Caper said. "She's not a lot older than I am, and I guarantee you that there's almost nothing on the internet about me."

"But you were a…" Micah trailed off.

"Criminal, you can say it out loud. My kid's aware, and also knows I'm doing my best to pay for those past mistakes and decisions. But that might tell us something. Is she someone else? Did she have a different name? A different life before this one that made her completely distance herself from the last? How long ago did she come here, and from where? You might want to have a chat with this Rick guy. Did he come with her, or did she meet him while here? Did she get a substantial loan for the business, or was it just a little something to be able to start building her credit with this new identity?"

By this time, Micah was scribbling furiously in his notebook, and I left him to it.

Caper had this in hand, and I was wondering if it was time to consult with the books again. There had to be something we were missing. Something that could at least show a crack in why she had been murdered, and then by extension, who would have done it. A path forward to break this thing wide open. And I wasn't going to get it here.

I waited to leave until they were done going over theories and came to the conclusion that more research was necessary. Once Mena had shown Micah to the front door, I turned to Caper and Isaac.

"Can you two do some deep diving on things? I have a theory of my own, but I have to go to the library to test it out." I rose from my chair and stood between them, both tall guys who felt like pillars.

"Yep, we'll do our thing, you go do your 'woo woo' stuff with the dead trees," Caper said with a smile.

I was so caught off guard that I guffawed and then slapped my hand over my mouth. Clearing my throat, I dropped my hand. "Nicely done. I'll have to remember that one."

Caper preened, and Isaac rolled his eyes as I left. I hadn't exactly expected to run into Mena out in the foyer, since I had figured she would have talked Micah into maybe going into the billiard room, or even to her room, before he left.

But I found her looking like one of those romantic movie heroines, standing at the window with her fingers spread on the window glass, as she gazed longingly after her beau.

"Really?" I said, because I couldn't help myself.

She turned and laughed. "You could just let me have my moment."

"Not likely."

"Doesn't matter. He saw me, and that was enough."

"I have to ask, are you playing him or yourself?"

"Nothing like having an older sister."

I scoffed. "You're lucky the oldest one isn't down here. It would have been much worse." I stroked her arm. "In all seriousness, though, do you actually like him?"

She sighed. "I do, and there's something there that keeps drawing me back to him over and over again. But I can't seem to find the place where I trust that it's actually going to work out. Not everyone magically gets a hint that the family of the guy you want in your life is connected, so you don't have to worry about closing off your gifts."

Ow. But I kept that to myself, because there really was some hurt there, and I didn't want to discount how she was feeling. "We still need to talk to the council. There aren't as many of us in the world as there used to be, and we're not doing anything wrong, so maybe it might be time to open things back up. We're not living during the Inquisition or the witch trials. With the internet, more and more people are interested in beliefs and systems they never even knew existed. Maybe it won't be a burst out into the open, throwing the door wide, or anything, but I think there should be something said for mixing with the non-talent-laden people of this world."

"I agree, but how do we do it?" She glanced back out at the driveway where Micah was motoring away in his squad car.

"Let's get this thing solved first, and then we'll put our collectively awesome and astute brains to it. We'll even rope Anjanetta in. She can't say no to both of us."

"Sure, I can. No." The oldest of the three of us came down the stairs in front of her husband.

Mena and I looked at each other and giggled like when we were younger.

"That's a sound I haven't heard in years," Anjanetta said, making her way down the rest of the stairs.

"You should visit more often. So far, Mena hasn't gone anywhere, even though I would have sworn she'd be gone and back to doggy-sitting duty shortly after she arrived last year." I hooked arms with one sister and waited for the other to join us.

"Your wayward ways are no longer onward ways, dear sister?" Anjanetta moved to stand on the other side of me so that we made a chain of oldest to youngest. I hadn't felt this connected and grounded in a very long time, and my mind started whirling with the possibilities. I'd save that for another day, but I had thoughts, and they might just have to be made into reality.

"I'm deciding," Mena said.

Anjanetta stepped to the left and hooked her arm through Mena's, making us a circle. We all bowed our heads so that our crowns were touching. It might have looked weird to those on the outside, but inside this circle, there was a magic that had nothing to do with talent and everything to do with love.

"You need to unshield, Philomena, if you truly desire what you think you want. He'll be hooked for life if you can make yourself let down that wall," Anjanetta said softly, then lifted her head and kissed each of us on our foreheads before stepping back.

"What about me?" I asked. "I want a prediction, too!" It was a running joke that if she provided for one, she had to provide for the other, so we didn't feel left out.

My oldest sister laughed and pinched my chin. "You are in for all kinds of trials and tribulations, but no one is more prepared, or capable, than you to weather these storms and come out on the other side looking like the best of rainbows."

"Does it have to be trials *and* tribulations? Can't I put a request in for one or the other?"

She closed her eyes for a moment, and when she opened them again, her gaze was laser-focused on me. "No, you'll do it all, and not only grow, but flourish under it. Your purpose here is bigger than I think you can comprehend, but I'll be interested to watch from the sidelines." She blinked and shook her head. "That's some powerful stuff there, Roxy. Brace yourself while Mena and I get the popcorn."

Well, that didn't make me feel much better about my situation, but if she had seen anything that would hurt me or stretch me beyond my limits, she would have said something. She had in high school, and I had not taken her seriously. There was no popcorn for that incident, and we didn't talk much about it, but I often wished I had listened to her. Not that I told her that, since her ego was already big enough, but the thought was there.

Not to mention that if we needed an advocate to the higher-ups about this magic mixing thing, I might have just been staring at our very best version of a crusader.

I put the idea in the back of my brain as I waved Anjanetta and Clive out the door. They were walking around town and exploring for the day, then taking the ferry across the river to do the same on the other side.

"It's going to be okay," Mena said, keeping her arm hooked with mine. "I can eat popcorn and help at the same time."

"Thanks a lot," I said.

"Always here to help, Roxy. You know that."

And I did. Now I just needed to see what kind of help I needed so I could send everyone out to comb the town for who had actually killed a woman who had no history past ten years ago.

Chapter 17

I left Mena staring out the window and finally made it to the library. I had business to conduct, and it would be much easier if I were on my own so I could concentrate and hopefully ask the right questions.

Browsing the different sections I'd set up and moved around when I'd first taken over the inn, I tried to look at the big picture first. Poobah had done a good enough job of shelving the many thousands of books we had in the two-story room. But he had not had the same panache as I did when it came to making sure each section was well represented, and full of the very best, and sometimes the very worst, of what the literary world had to offer.

I'd even made little signs for each section from engraving plates I'd found in the basement, too.

I brushed my fingers along the spines of the books in the adventure section, hoping for something to spark to help me out. It would have been so much easier if I could just say a question and get a distinct and specific answer, but that was never going to actually happen. Having a talent could make it easier, certainly, but it didn't make it infallible.

Pity.

Life would have been so much easier if it had.

But, alas, I was stuck wandering and hoping. Normally, I could just grab a book, ask the question, then flip the book open to a page and blindly choose a paragraph. I'd read it and get the meaning out of it through the feeling and interpretation of the words. But with all the practicing I'd been doing under the guidance of Aunt Hellen and Uncle Vince, things had started to glow, even when it didn't involve a murder or trouble. And that was better handled if I found the right book, at the right time, instead of just randomly.

This required me to often wander through this lovely library while projecting my questions. I would jokingly say I was taking one for the team, but it certainly wasn't a hardship. I would have been here every day at every hour if I could. In fact, I had been, as a teenager, helping around the inn when Poobah and Grand Duchess, or Duchy, had owned and run the thing.

I missed her on the daily.

Shaking my head, I got back to my question. I couldn't just ask who had killed Emma because I wouldn't get a helpful answer. I had to ask broader or more nuanced questions to get to the place where I could then start on the journey to figuring things out on my own. I had thought this was a useless talent, so frivolous compared to what other people could do. But when it came to sleuthing, it had been the biggest help. I only hoped it would do the same this time, especially since it was my head on the chopping block against a nefarious cop who had it out for me, instead of just one who didn't like me.

Perhaps that was where I should start. What was going on with Chief Grady Morony? And, really, was there any more apt a name for him? I'd looked it up to see its origins and was interested to find that it was actually an Irish name. Which gelled with his family being in line with the talent, though they apparently no longer had access to it, according to Chief Moron.

I snickered, even though I shouldn't have. Although there was no one in here with me, it wasn't like I was going to get questioned on how I could laugh at such a serious time.

"How can you laugh at such a serious time?" Poobah came in through the double doors of the library as if he were being propelled by a steam train.

I didn't even waste the effort of rolling my eyes, especially because a book had just started glowing on the second level, which meant I would get to use my very favorite piece of the library, the rolling ladder.

But it would have to wait because Poobah had storm clouds racing across his face, and what little hair he had left was standing straight up from his balding head.

I immediately sedated myself and got down to business. Something was wrong here, and it wouldn't help anyone if I joked around about it.

"What did you find?" I asked.

"It's what I didn't find." He flipped his trusty tablet open and secured the cover with the elastic. After that, he kicked out the stand and set it on one of the long tables I'd put in the library for people who wanted to study or spread out their newspaper or do a puzzle.

I almost asked if he'd prepared a PowerPoint and if he wanted the projector up. But even that would have ridden the line too close to making light of whatever was bothering him.

"There was something about this whole thing that troubled me ever since you told me about the way Emma died. I never had much to do with floral things, but your grandmother would often send me into the store to pick up whatever she had ordered. I spoke with Rick far more than I ever did with Emma, as she seemed to be in the back of the store working or out of the store doing something else. But Taboo kept getting his paw stuck in his collar when he was scratching, and I happened to look at the tag. There was something about that one side that caught my attention. A symbol. One I couldn't place. Until I went through Duchy's diaries."

My mind was racing with so many questions, and the fact that about thirteen books had started throwing sparkles throughout the room in different sections. Even the board game closet seemed to be glowing. What the heck was going on?

I closed my eyes for a moment and reached out to grab Poobah's arm for support. He gave it without question and led me to sit down in one of the chairs at the table.

"Breathe. Whatever is happening is okay, and we'll get through it. In and out, Roxy. Process one thing at a time."

"I'm trying," I squeaked out. The connection with him was helping, though, and I was able to get my bearings back. "Okay." I breathed in and out. "Okay. I don't know what just happened, but it was like the whole place lit up with fireworks for the finale on the island during the Fourth."

"Interesting," he said, his hand still on mine where I had a death grip on his forearm.

"That's probably going to leave a mark." I tried to loosen my grip, but he held me tight with his aging hand.

"Just stay still for a second. There's something here, but we both need to take a moment to recenter and ground ourselves before we try to move forward."

"I did that earlier."

"We need to do it again. Just stay still with me for a few seconds."

So, I stayed still for a few seconds with Poobah, my anchor in so many things. Our breathing came in tandem, in and out rhythmically. My heart stopped racing, my hands stopped shaking, and my mind cleared.

Poobah took a few seconds longer, and I waited for him to release my hand and then pat it before opening my eyes. The sparkles were still there, but not quite as bright, not quite as chaotic, not quite as many, more manageable. Rising from the chair, I went to the thirteen different spots that were ignited and pulled the various books from the shelves that were glowing. Using the keys at my waist, I opened the puzzle closet, then pulled out the puzzle box covered in a giant Ferris wheel. I set it on the table with all the other treasures. It was a favorite and had probably been put together over a hundred times during the thirty years we'd had it.

There was no rhyme or reason to how these all connected, but I felt better about having them all out and ready to open.

"Before we dive into this, let me tell you what I found, and why that symbol struck a memory with me that had me pulling out Duchy's journals."

"Okay." My fingers itched to get into those books, and especially the puzzle. But Poobah was older and wiser on many fronts, and he knew more about all of this than I did. Plus, it never hurts to have as much information as possible before taking the leap into the magical.

"There was a young girl who was brought to us at the inn many years ago. Her father wanted her cleansed."

"Cleansed?" I hadn't ever heard that term before.

"It's what some people think needs to be done if they find that a child can do things they aren't supposed to do, or if they have tendencies that don't run in the same line as the community's beliefs."

"I don't like the sound of that. By community, do you mean something religious?"

"Religion is a whole other thing than what this community was." He sighed. "I didn't pay much attention because I thought it was a father with a young teenager who was just being a teenager and doing teenage things. But Duchy felt the need to cleanse her, or at least tell her father she'd cleansed her. And then they went on their way, and we didn't see them again."

"So, they weren't from around here?" This was fascinating, but I didn't understand how it all related to Emma's death, except that Poobah had said it was a symbol he'd seen on Taboo's collar that had triggered the memory. Did that mean...

"After seeing the symbol and matching it to the picture your grandmother took and pasted into her journal, I'm wondering if Emma was the teenager. That wasn't her name at the time. It was Aspen, and we never saw her again. Perhaps someone from her past has found her? Duchy had been concerned with there being some kind of cult, at least that's what she wrote in her journal. But when she called the police, there was nothing they could do. She wasn't injured, she appeared healthy, and we didn't have her whole name. Just her first, and we only knew the man who brought her to us as Father."

It was definitely something to think about. Especially since I wasn't hearing about anyone in town that had a grudge with her, despite the lie I told Chief Moron that there were plenty of people who might have had a grudge against her. And, it would also give a hint as to why she had no records before ten years ago.

"Maybe the books have something to say about that. Can I look now with this new information?"

"Of course, thank you for waiting. I just felt like it was important you know that before we dive into all your sparkles. Not that I see them, though I wish I did. It must be something to have that kind of light show go off every time there's information you need."

I laughed because that was only half of it. "It can be cool to see the light show, but I never get any concrete answers, just a bunch of clues to point me in the right direction."

"That's far more than I get sometimes. I'll ask the cards a question about the weather, and they will give me a plum sitting high in a tree with a ladder below it. What am I supposed to do with that?"

I'd seen that card before when he was doing pulls, and it made me giggle. I wasn't just a plum. It was a plum with facial features, holding a rake, sitting in a tree with its legs dangling to the branch below. I had no way to interpret that, no matter what the question was. Okay, so maybe my talent was cleaner when it came to helping, but I also needed to see the clues this time to get myself on track.

I flipped open the first book and a trail of glitter rose above the pages, but then hung there without forming any words. I flipped open the next book, and it did the same thing. In fact, every book was opened on the big table with a cloud of sparkles over each, until I opened the puzzle, and suddenly things started moving at the speed of light.

I held my breath and Poobah's hand as they began settling into a pattern. "Can you write this down, please? I don't know if I'll be able to keep it all in my head until it's done."

"Of course." He didn't let me go as he grabbed a piece of paper from the cubby under the table, then pulled a pen out of the neck of his shirt.

"Green. Crowded. Beware. Fortune." I paused because usually I got phrases, not just single words. But more were popping up over the books. "Creature. Dating. Happy. Ruin. Light. Justice." What the heck was all this? "Close. Marriage. Renewal. Secrets." All the words stayed hanging above their books. I closed the one with Justice over it to see if the title of the book had anything to do with the message, but it was a book on fixing cars, so no. Okay then.

Glancing over at Poobah, I saw that he was still scribbling. After another thirty seconds, I verified that he had all the right words. But what did they all mean? I was used to getting at least some feeling about what the message meant or a thought on the direction in which to answer the posed questions with the phrase I was given. That seemed to have totally gone out the window over the last several days. Instead, I got warnings about chasms and lies and that the time was nigh. I was pretty certain that the weary traveler was Willow, and that at least made sense, but not the rest of what messages I'd been given. So frustrating!

I was about to bust out with some serious swear words about the state of chaos this was throwing everything into when the puzzle jumped on the table, and all the pieces spilled out, then started arranging themselves like one of those stop-motion movies I loved. And it wasn't the picture on the front of the box.

Chapter 18

The puzzle kept creating itself on the table with no help from anyone I could see. Since we did have one ghost who resided at the inn, I couldn't say there were no such things as ghosts, and therefore, it couldn't be one of them. But I was pretty sure I would have at least seen a hand moving the pieces around if, in fact, it was being helped along.

But it wasn't, that I could tell. I glanced at Poobah just to check if he was seeing the same thing I was seeing.

"Has this ever happened before?" I asked when I found him as dumbfounded as I was.

"Can't say I've seen it if it has. What do you think it's creating?"

"I was hoping you might know."

"Your hopes are bound to be dashed then because I am completely clueless." He tucked his hands into the pockets of his pants as we both stood there waiting for whatever was about to emerge from the picture on the table.

The corners were built out. The colors were in for the grass and a blue sky. The click of the pieces coming together was almost hypnotic as they shifted and set down in a continuous spiral, and each one was set, and the next was chosen. The picture on the outlying boundaries was complete. The inner pieces were being put down in circle after circle, spiraling toward the middle to complete the thing. And yet, I still had no idea what exactly we were looking at.

I tried to clear my mind of any expectations. I didn't want to miss anything because I was looking for something else. But that didn't mean a stray thought or two didn't pop up. Was it a portrait? Would it reveal the killer in full color? Was there something within the outer edges of the picture that would gel with the inner depths of the picture? Was this going to confuse me even more?

That last one was truly valid, though, because so far this murder mystery had far more complications and arms than I had experienced before. Not that the others had been straightforward, but in the end, they'd clicked into place like the pieces of the puzzle, and ultimately made sense.

Right now, there were so many different moving parts with the paper burning, the plethora of sparkling books with no concrete message, and the chief who was after me for no other reason than he thought I had what he wanted.

But how did they all come together?

The picture started filling in with a green that looked like it was dappled with sunlight. The bottom was green, but also a lot of brown, gray, and white. Some darkness filtered in as the pieces coalesced in the picture. The middle filled in an inch at a time.

"What do you think this is?" I asked after finally finding my voice.

"I have an idea what it might be, but I don't know that it makes sense. Let's wait to see what it is at the end. It's almost done."

And it was. As it came closer and closer to the middle, it picked up speed, clicking like someone who could type at ninety-five words per minute.

Then it was done. And I was a little confused as to what I was looking at. Not the actual picture, since that was definitely three trees standing together in the middle of a meadow. The sky was an amazing palette of blue and shades of white in the clouds. Below the grass was an undulating green with the darker colors mixed in, a base for the three trees to take root in. There was a tree with yellow leaves and a white trunk, one with the long tendrils of green leaves, and the third had a dark green top with a network of roots above the ground.

So, an aspen tree, a willow, and a cypress tree. But what did it mean?

As I opened my mouth to ask Poobah, I kept my gaze roving over the picture again and again. And that was when it hit me.

"Didn't you say the girl whose father came to you was named Aspen?"

"Yes." He drew out the word as he probably was thinking things through, too.

"And Willow just showed up last night."

"She did…" He trailed off in a way that signaled he was trying to get on the same page with me.

Poking the puzzle to see if it would stay intact, I traced the roots of the third tree. "Cypress." I grabbed my phone out of my pocket and took a quick shot of the whole thing so I could look over it more later.

"It is."

"So, if you've met Aspen in the past, and Willow in the present, then is Cypress someone we should be looking for in the future?" The puzzle jumped like the small piece of paper had done on the pool table. If this thing burst into flames, I did not know what I would do with myself.

It didn't burst, though. It simply shattered, the pieces all scattering away from each other and changing colors before my very eyes. I'd put this puzzle of a Ferris wheel together at least fifty times in my life. Looking down at the pile of pieces, they now reflected what I had come to expect from the box, and not a tree in sight.

"Well, then," I said, glancing over at Poobah. He had a look on his face that I couldn't decipher.

"Exactly."

"At the risk of repeating myself again, what the heck does this mean?"

He sifted through the pile of puzzle pieces that had changed to their original form. "I think it means we have to find this Cypress."

"Like we need another mystery." I sounded grumpy with those words, but I wasn't going to apologize for it. "Where do we even start? It could be someone from long ago. Someone we haven't met yet. Or someone we know who no longer has the same name as they did before, since both Willow and Aspen went by other names when they were younger."

"That's a very astute observation." He moved around the table. "I think it might be time to get your board up and begin the process of not only listing everything out that we have, but also starting to make some of the connections. There was something in the picture that we're missing. I'm so glad you got a photo of it, though. Print it out and put it in the middle of the board. I have a few things to verify, and you've sent everyone else out to do things. It might be time to start collating all the info and see what we have to work with."

I sighed because he was right, quashing my tiny wish for a few minutes without something new to do.

But I wanted the board, and I wanted the answers, so a rest right now was not going to happen, regardless of what I wanted.

After leaving the library, we said goodbye at the door to my downstairs rooms. Taboo had started making the room his own with a dog bed, a water station, and several toys. I hadn't heard anything new about Rick or his hospital stay, but I'd sent Aunt Hellen to check that out.

The rooms had been mostly cleaned out, but I had originally considered making them my office, so that I no longer worked where I lived, or at least not having to sleep in the same room where I wrote the checks and balanced the books.

So, there was a desk in here, along with a long table and a printer.

I got down to the business of printing out everything we had, including pictures of the shop, and of Taboo, and the puzzle. I added in a few pictures of Rick, as well, but had absolutely no luck in finding a single piece of photographic evidence that Emma had ever existed.

I'd even gone back as far as the grand opening of Petal Paradise when she'd cut the ribbon with her back to the camera. I would have thought it was a mistake, or a blooper, if I had been able to find any other pictures of her face, but there were none.

Even the pictures of various events either had her not in them at all, or if she did get captured on film, it was her back or from the side, with her face completely turned away from the camera. Was she hiding? Why hadn't she chosen to be something that was far less customer-facing if she didn't want to be found?

Another question that went up on another notecard I would need to tack to my big board, once I got it out from the basement. I'd stored it down there last year, thinking I would not need it again. So many questions, and so few answers, but I had hope that I'd start getting info to link together soon, once I got the board up.

Which meant a trip to the basement. I could have sent Dean or Isaac, but I was already in motion and could get it myself. Plus, I could check in with Earl, our resident ghost. Poobah had said he'd talked with him earlier today, but with all the preparations for the wedding, even with Sharon's help, my days had been very full. Per Poobah, the ghost would have let me know if he'd needed something, and I hadn't heard from him, so he should be good. But if I was going to be in his domain, the least I could do was see how he was passing the time.

Poobah had said before that Earl sometimes went into a kind of hibernating period where he wouldn't come out for months or years on end. Made sense if you'd been in the same place for decade after decade after century. He did enjoy interacting with Amelia, though, and so he still used the phone booth under the stairs when she dropped her coins in the slot.

The door to the basement was locked, per usual, so I used the keys at my waist to gain entry. We had quite a bit of inventory down here, along with our entire wine cellar. Some bottles were almost as old as the inn itself.

Walking down the narrow stairs, I tried to run through if there was anything else I needed from down here. Since we had so many people on-site, it would make sense to also check our supply of bubbly to celebrate Willow's return. I considered shooting off a quick text to Glennis to see if she was willing to make another dinner tonight. Although we could probably all exist on leftovers at this point. I'd cleared it with Caper and his family earlier. I knew that they were setting up house down at the cottage, but a meal to overwrite the one earlier when Norm had come in with his angry face would be nice. And he'd better not show up again, or I was going to seriously have some words with him, and they wouldn't be the nice ones.

Once I arrived at the bottom of the stairs, I looked around and found the bottles of champagne, making a note to send Dean down after them later. We had several hours until dinner anyway, and he was upstairs unpacking.

I went through the room and then entered the warren of hallways and spaces under the huge inn. There were rooms of cleaning supplies, others with linens and extra pillows, another of holiday decorations, and yet one more that was filled with all manner of party supplies for any occasion. We did a brisk business here at The Charmed Inn for family reunions, birthday celebrations, weddings, and anniversary parties, as well as retreats and conferences. We also had a number of people who had more private celebrations, with just a partner, or some kind of life event where they wanted a little fanfare just for them personally. We were able to fulfill that need, too. Each event had different needs, and having everything on hand already meant lower costs, but bigger fanfare. Just the way I liked it.

I wasn't sure which room the whiteboard had ended up in when Dean had brought it back down last year. We'd used a black slate board to direct people around for the wedding with lovely purple chalk. It was still upstairs, and I probably could have tried to use that, but the whiteboard had a panel of corkboard, and I wanted that. Slate could be ruined if I didn't use the right things to attach my findings to it.

I rounded the last corner, hoping to find it stacked up against a wall or in the farthest room, back under the library. When I entered the room, the big whiteboard caught my eye, but that was quickly overtaken by the sight of Earl pacing back and forth in front of an old vanity mirror with years and years of de-silvering. A faint outline of him showed up in the mirror as he walked back and forth, and I caught the frown on his face and the way he kept pulling at the edges of his tailored jacket.

I cleared my throat to get his attention, but that didn't work, so I called his name.

He halted in midstride. He actually floated as opposed to stepping along the floor, but he still made the steps as if he had an impact on the floor. It was quite a sight to see him with one leg lifted to take the next step onto air. I would have snickered, but he looked far too serious for that right now.

I remembered he had felt a spirit pass when Emma had died, so maybe he was worrying about that? I wasn't sure, and I wouldn't know until I asked.

"Are you okay?" I pushed the door closed behind me, just in case anyone else decided to walk into the bowels of the inn.

"Yes, yes, of course. I appreciate you asking." He went back to pacing.

"Is something bothering you? Is it something I can help with?"

He scoffed. "Bothering me? Nothing bothers a ghost when they've been dead this long. I've made peace with my past for the most part, thanks to you, and I find myself mildly amused by the young girl upstairs who has more questions than anyone I've ever encountered before. She truly is a delight, even if she often strains my knowledge to the very brink. She found a new number to call recently. All nines, she said. It's simply a recording of old songs from the aughts, so I told her that was fine to do."

I smiled because Amelia did that to nearly everyone in her orbit. "As long as you feel it's legitimate, that's fine. But what about you? What has you pacing?"

"There's something here. Something..." He reached out his hand and touched the mirror, or, at least, seemed to touch the mirror, though he wouldn't be able to do anything with his see-through fingers and hand. "Something here. I know it, I remember it, I feel it, but there's something here, and I can't get to it. There's a door here somewhere."

"A door?"

"Yes, Roxy, a door. I know for a fact I do not stutter."

"Okay, a door. But how can there be a door when we're at the back of the inn? This is under the library, and there's nothing beyond that."

He huffed out a sigh. "I do understand, but I can feel it, and yet somehow I can't see it. How is that possible?"

"You're asking the wrong person. Why don't you try walking through the wall and see if that would take you where you think you need to go?"

"You think I haven't tried that?"

I shrugged because there was no good answer to that question that wouldn't lead him to being more irritated with me, and I was not a fan of an irritated Earl, especially when I had other things to do.

"Is the door behind the vanity?"

"I'm not certain. All I know is that the room behind this door has been calling to me for years, and I've never been able to find it. But lately, I keep getting pulled back here to this room and this vanity in particular, so I believe this is where it is."

Somehow that made sense, and instead of waiting around and doing more questions and answers, I put my hands on the end of the table, my back into it, and shoved the vanity down a foot. And lo and behold, there was a door back there. It was narrow, like a linen closet door, but it was definitely a door. And it definitely had a knob and a keyhole.

I rattled the knob, and there was no budging it. "I'm guessing it's locked."

"I'm guessing you're not Sherlock," he shot back, and I smiled at his irritation this time.

"I'm the one who would have the key, so you might want to be a little nicer to me if you want me to see if I can unlock the door. Or you could try floating through it first."

"I don't tend to float through things, thank you very much. I open them like a normal person, much like the wine rack that my other room is hidden behind, if you'll remember."

"Of course, I remember. It's where I got a lot of the furniture for the third floor and to redo my office. And before you say anything, I've made sure nothing has been taken off the premises."

"At least you listened to me for that instance."

I could have harrumphed at him, but I chose not to. "I need to get this board upstairs. Why don't you move the vanity the rest of the way?"

"You think I haven't tried moving it all?"

"I have no idea of what you have and haven't done, and I have things to do. Do you want me to move it for you, or are you going to try to go through the wall?" I hitched the board up. It was getting heavy.

"Perhaps." He took a few steps back, even though he probably didn't have to, and then he hurled himself at the door.

Both comically and unfortunately, he bounced off it like someone had thrown a bouncy ball at a brick wall. Interesting.

Chapter 19

Earl shook his head, then ran a hand through his now tousled hair. I had never seen him so disheveled before and stunned. When he stumbled backward, I reached out a hand to steady him without thinking. It went right through his arm instead of making contact, because of course it did. He was a ghost.

His stumble had him landing against the door again and coming to a full stop.

"I don't want you to hurt yourself, but is the full wall what you can't get through, or just the door?"

"It doesn't hurt, necessarily. It's just jarring."

I put the whiteboard down against the wall I was talking about and grabbed the keys from my waist. There had to be one on here that would open the door. I sorted through all the keys that I knew what they went to—from the kitchen to the linen closet upstairs, to the new lock we'd put on the door to the third floor so that it could remain our domain alone.

There were a couple of keys that would have collected dust if they hadn't been on the ring I always carried with me. I tried the first three, and none of them fit. I tried the other five, which I wasn't even sure of their purpose, and they didn't fit either.

Earl paced next to me. I wanted to tell him to stop so I could concentrate, but figured it wouldn't do any good. Instead, I tried the last key, and that was a miss, too.

"Hmmm. None of these are the right one."

"I could have told you that," Earl said, resting his hand against the wood.

"Do you have to want to go through something for it to happen?" I asked, thinking about how he didn't sink through the floor when he was upstairs. Something had to keep him from just melting into this wall or that against his will. He could move furniture and certain things when he put his mind to it, which made it a valid question.

He sighed anyway and then answered in a voice that held some serious irritation. "You think I haven't thought of that?"

"You don't have to be nasty."

He bowed his head as he blew out a breath. I had never asked if he actually breathed, since I didn't think that was a nice question, and I let it go this time, too, because it would only make things worse.

"My deepest apologies for not saying that in a more pleasant way. This room has been calling me for some time, and I haven't been able to get in. I will forget about it for a short time, and then it will begin calling me again. I don't know what is in there. I would like to understand why it keeps tempting me now, and what is in there that keeps pulling at me like it hasn't in all the years I've been here."

"Oh, I didn't realize that. How long is for some time?"

His laugh was rounded out with a scoff. "I was trying to think about that just yesterday, actually, and I couldn't come up with an answer that made sense. Time is incredibly fluid for me, being that I've been here for decades and decades. A day or a year can be the same, depending on what's going on. Of course, time has seemed far more solid and slow with you at the helm, but that could be for a number of different reasons."

Leave it to Earl to take a dig, even as he was wanting something from me.

"I can go ask Aunt Hellen and Poobah if there are any other keys I don't know about. If the door is locked, then it has to have a way to unlock it. Barring that, I have a few other ideas." I left it, and Earl, there as I was contemplating asking Caper to pick the lock on the door, but I didn't want to tempt him with doing bad things. Then again, I was the owner and would be the one asking him to do it, so it wasn't like it would be against the law.

I decided to think about it as I walked up the stairs with my big murder board. Like I needed another mystery. But I figured this one should be relatively easy to take care of, and then it would be off my plate. And as far as I was concerned, Earl would owe me another favor. That worked for me.

I hiked up the last few steps, dragging the board behind me, then kept the board from sailing down the stairs with my hip as I opened the door at the top into the lobby. I should have thought this through before I'd headed down on my own, but I'd just have to remember that for next time.

Fortunately, when I entered the lobby, Aunt Hellen was at the front desk, one less person I'd have to run down. I was taking my wins where I could get them.

"Do we have any extra keys that aren't on my ring?" I asked her.

She bit her lip and shuffled a few things around on the desk. "Not that I know of. Why do you ask?"

"There's a door downstairs Earl has been trying to get into, but he can't. He even tried to throw himself against it, and he bounced off like a rubber ball instead of sailing through as he normally would anywhere else."

"That's strange." She stopped shuffling and looked up at me. "What's in the room?"

"I have no idea. That's why I wanted to see if there's a key. I honestly can't remember ever seeing the door before, but there are so many in the basement that it's possible I just never noticed it."

"Maybe check in with your Poobah. He could have a key, maybe." She went back to shuffling.

"Are you looking for something in particular? I wasn't expecting you to work today, so I was going to come find you before dinner."

"Is there a dinner tonight?"

"Not really." I shrugged. "I was going to see if there was something we could throw into the oven if no one has plans. The week is a little different from what I had originally thought it was going to be, but everyone is still here, and I want to go over a few things."

Her head snapped up. "Speaking of that..."

I waited a second, but she didn't continue. "Yes?"

"I was able to get over to the hospital, and Rick wasn't there. He'd checked himself out a few hours before. Did he ever show up here?"

"No. Did he pick up Taboo at least?"

As if in answer to his name, the animal in question came bouncing around the corner with Poobah close behind him.

"I'll take that as a no," I said.

"No, Rick has not yet come by to pick up the dog, but Taboo has made a friend, and I don't know how we're going to separate them when the time comes."

And to add to the filling room, Daffy Daffodil came trotting around the corner, her short legs not keeping up with man and bigger beast, but still obviously happy to be in the crowd. Her tail was wagging like no one's business, and the little smile on her face was absolutely adorable. Taboo sat at the right side of the desk, and Daffy joined him there, also sitting, but a whole lot shorter than her new best friend.

I laughed and petted both of them. "Amelia let you take her dog?"

"Only while she's in the phone booth."

"Is she talking to Earl? Because I was down there a little while ago, and he seems to have found a door I don't have a key to." Might as well hit all the nails at the same time with one hammer.

"Yes, she and Earl are in cahoots about something. And before you get your dander up, I assure you it's nothing bad." He took a seat on the couch in the lobby. "These two, or three, are wearing me out."

I laughed again because it was good for him to be worn out. He'd let go of the inn a few years after Duchy had died and said he was retiring fully, but I was of a mind that he still needed to be active and not hide away from the world. This at least got him out and about and kept him around the inn, which I loved.

"Take a rest then, but about the door."

"Right, the door. Where is it and what does it go to? As far as I've ever known, all keys are on that ring at your waist. I don't know of a single door that can't be opened."

"Well, this one can't, and how does a door just appear out of nowhere? That's not possible. We must have something somewhere that will open it."

"Or I'm sure that you've considered asking Caper to pick the lock." Poobah gave me a sly look, and I blushed because I definitely had thought of it. "I'm sure he'd be happy to keep his talents up and running."

"I don't want to tempt him."

There was a laugh from the dining room doorway, and then Willow came strolling in. "You don't have to worry about the temptation thing, Roxy. Caper deliberately locks himself out of rooms simply to pick the lock. The man is trying his hardest not to do the wrong thing, but he has some issues. Ones I hope to help with now that I'm here. But there are some I'm not going to be able to keep him from doing."

It was quite a full lobby now with the two dogs, my aunt, my grandfather, Amelia in the phone booth under the stairs, probably dialing her nines, and Willow standing in the archway of the dining room. I found myself absolutely overwhelmed with gratitude and happiness that each part of the family was here, and the glow of the room increased with that togetherness.

This was the life, and I hoped it only got better. I'd have to stay out of jail, though, for it to do that. Which reminded me...

"I'm going to throw something together for dinner tonight so that we can meet and go over everything that we have." I shook my head and sighed. "Anything that we have at this point, since we seem not to have much to go on."

"Um, let's rethink the whole you cooking thing," Poobah said, tapping his chin. "I know you're going to look in the refrigerator or freezer and come up with something, but Glennis has a very strict way of stocking things, and we don't want to irritate her. She's been in a good mood since last year. Let's not mess with that. I'll order from Lucia's and let everyone know."

I wasn't going to fight with him, since he was absolutely correct in his assessment of my skills, or lack thereof. I was going to direct what was going to be on the table, though. "Make sure you get the stromboli I can't get enough of."

"Already on it. And while I'm out, I'm going to see if I can get in touch with a friend of Emma's who used to work at the shop. Maybe we can then have some more of that information you want, along with delicious food. I don't want to get caught out if that chief decides to send anyone here again. We need to solve this and get it done."

"Absolutely. Aunt Hellen, can you check on Rick again?"

"Yep, it's on my list of things to do. I tried calling the flower shop, but no one is answering, and the machine said they'd be closed for a few days. He has to be somewhere, though, if he's not there."

"Maybe Mrs. Lincoln has seen him. Check in with her and Fonzy." The whole world seemed to be running according to the dogs. Of course, that was when Moose came strolling into the lobby, then sat himself down between the two dogs who had decided to lie down curled next to each other. It was a menagerie, and I was in love with the picture they made.

"Okay, so we have a plan for the next few hours. I'll let Dean know if everyone else can let their family counterparts know. Poobah, if you'll communicate with Mena, Anjanetta, and Mom, then we'll all know what's happening, and it's time for a meet-up to exchange info. I have the board, so I'll get that set up before the dinner hour." It was a lot to consider, but I felt like Poobah did—that time was running out, and it would only take another visit from the cops to put me in a position I very much did not want to be in. I had to be proactive this time, not reactive, and the only way that was going to happen was if I went all in. The mystery of the key could wait a little, but the mystery of the cursed chocolate and the door locking behind me at Petal Paradise, as well as who had killed Emma, all needed answers. They were linked. They had to be. And if I could unravel one small part of the story, I had a feeling the rest would come tumbling out into the light.

"We have our orders then." Poobah looked at Willow. "Can Taboo stay here with you while I run my errands? I think it'll be easier since I'm just going to walk, and I can't take him into the restaurant?"

"Of course. I wonder why his owner hasn't come to get him yet. Is he still in the hospital?" Willow reached a hand down to scritch Taboo's head.

"No, not according to Aunt Hellen. That's strange, though. I thought we would have been his first stop when he checked himself out."

"Rick is not always the most reliable of people," Aunt Hellen said, and Poobah grunted. What was that all about?

"Well, hopefully he'll remember this is where he should be because I'd like to talk with him about Emma, too, and if we can do it here, then maybe my questions won't seem so intrusive," Poobah said.

There was a knock on the door behind me, and Poobah stiffened.

"Speak of the devil," he said.

"And he'll appear," Aunt Hellen finished.

Chapter 20

The door wasn't locked, but I did appreciate Rick knocking instead of just barging in without a reservation. Looking out through the glass as I turned the knob, I smiled at the older man. I wasn't sure what Poobah and Aunt Hellen had against him. I'd always found him to be pleasant when I interacted with him, and as far as I knew, he and Emma had a good relationship. Maybe he was just so steeped in grief he'd forgotten the dog. We were about to find out.

He entered with a smile and his hands in his pockets. Stopping in the doorway, he started visually making the rounds of all the people and animals in the lobby. "Quite a welcoming committee. And there's my boy, Taboo." He came further into the room with his hand outstretched towards his dog.

His dog, which bared his teeth.

Rick stopped in his tracks, put his hands back in his pockets, and took in the rest of the people in the room. As his gaze roved in the direction of the dining room, he drew in a breath. "Oh, Will..." He gulped then glanced at Poobah. "Will you, um, help me a little longer with keeping Taboo? There seems to be some question as to what Emma wanted when she passed, and I've been trying to sort things out. I'd really appreciate it if you could keep him a little longer while I do that sorting. Great, thanks!"

he said, then ducked out of the lobby without waiting for an answer or making eye contact with anyone else.

I was stunned enough with his abrupt departure that he had a chance to slam the front door, jump in his car, and roar out of the driveway before I had taken even one step to catch him.

We all heard the revving engine and screeching tires, though. I looked around the room to see if anyone knew what had just happened, because I certainly didn't.

"Do not let him back in here, and under no circumstances is he to take Taboo until I have more information," Poobah said, removing his keys from his pocket. "I believe there's quite a bit more going on here than I originally would have thought. I'd call Norm and tell him Rick just ran for no reason, and let him know I'm going to see if I can find out where he's going."

"Are you sure that's safe?" I asked.

"I'm only going to follow him if I can. I won't confront him, but keep your phone on for updates." And then he was out the door. Taboo lifted his head and did a little cry, but Daffy scooted closer, so their backs touched, and he quieted down. Even though it dislodged Moose a little, my cat did not seem to mind at all.

As I took my phone out to text Norm the info, Aunt Hellen and I looked at each other, and then we both glanced at Willow. There was something about the way Rick had asked his question, and then ran with no real reason. No one had said anything to him. No one had entered the room after he'd come in whom he would have been scared of. And yet, he'd run. The only difference from any other encounter here was Willow.

Willow, who was still standing near the doorway. But her face had gone from the sunny smile when she was talking about watching Taboo for Poobah, to her now gripping the frame of the door so hard that her knuckles were ashen colored.

I didn't run to her. Different people reacted differently to sudden movement, and I found it better to ease into a situation like this. She looked much like she had when she'd seen the sparkles fly out of the cookbook, which I still had to go try to get to talk to me again. But that was a thought for another time.

Right now, Willow looked like she wanted to run, but something held her rooted to the spot. Her hand on the doorframe?

"Are you okay?" I asked her when I was about four feet in front of her. Should I call Caper? See if I could get Amelia to come out of the phone booth to help soothe her mom? What was the right call here?

Aunt Hellen decided it was yanking one of the chairs from behind the desk and shoving it toward the woman. As soon as it was positioned right, Willow dropped back into the chair. But her wide-eyed and confused expression didn't change.

"Maybe we should call Caper?" I said out loud this time.

It must have snapped something for Willow to break her stasis, because she immediately started shaking her head violently. "No, no, please don't call Caper just yet. I need a minute. I just saw a ghost, so I need a minute."

I looked behind me to see if she meant Earl, but he was nowhere to be found. Glancing at Aunt Hellen, I quirked an eyebrow, and she shrugged.

"Take your minute. We're here when you're ready." I was not always very good with patience, but I was going to have to be outwardly this time. Inwardly, though, I was connecting dots that seemed like they shouldn't even be in the same universe, much less in the same timeline. Was Rick someone she had known previously? Where and when? Had she thought he was dead?

For her part, Willow sat with her head bowed and blew out a long breath very slowly. She gripped her knees, not as hard as she'd done with the doorframe, but still enough to make indentations right below her shorts line.

I stopped wondering about what this could all mean and started focusing fully on the woman before me. I'd been told we'd get a weary traveler, and as much as I had thought it was her, I don't know that I had considered why she would be weary, or if the weariness could happen after she got here, instead of bringing it with her.

I did know that the day in the house with her husband and kids and having meals with us had given her a glow she had been missing when she showed up at my door. That glow was completely gone now, replaced by a kind of darkness I hoped we could shine a light on. As soon as she was ready to tell us why she felt like she'd seen a ghost.

I took a step closer to her just in case she fainted and fell out of the chair. Aunt Hellen shook her head abruptly and showed me her phone with Caper's profile pulled up and a text chain going.

Five seconds later, the French doors in the dining room were wrenched open, and then there was Caper, down on one knee in front of his wife.

"Whatever it is, whatever happened, we can fix it. I know we can. Do you need to go lie down? Is there something I can do? Help me help you."

Willow released one knee to cup Caper's jaw. "There's nothing you can do. I just have to sort through things in my mind to be able to put it into words." She looked up at Aunt Hellen. "Thank you for contacting him."

Aunt Hellen nodded, and I was still waiting for whatever was going to come next. This was big, whatever it was. I just didn't know how big.

Finally, Willow nodded and lifted her chin. "Okay, I'm ready. I'm sorry that I made such a scene. That's so unlike me." She stood, and Caper stood with her. "I'm almost positive that man used to be in the compound where I was raised. We were all told he died years ago and that his life and his sin were a caution to the rest of us to not step out of line."

Compound? Sin?

"You're sure it was him?" Caper asked.

"Not positive. It's been about twenty years since I last saw him. But the tattoo under his ear is right, and while he hasn't exactly aged well, he also looks almost exactly as he did before, just with more lines in his face." She closed her eyes and cleared her throat. "There are things I haven't told you, or rather things I told you that weren't completely true," she said to Caper and Caper alone. "I can pack my bags tonight and be gone by morning. I don't want to bring anything bad here. I thought I was out, but now I'm not so sure."

"You're not packing your bags." Three voices, all the same words, different tones, but the sentiment was the same.

The power in the three of us could have been akin to a spell. Willow stumbled back into her husband's arms, and then she cried while laughing at the exact same time. That was a skill I might have to figure out how to master.

Honestly, it was better than letting her run.

She patted Caper's arm that was snaked around her waist and sighed. "Okay, then, I'm going to assume I don't have to guess how you all feel about this one."

"Not even for a millisecond," I said. "But I would like to hear why you think Rick is the same person, and why you said you thought you had gotten out of something, but now you're not sure. What was that something?"

She tried to step away from Caper, but he was having none of it. He didn't cage her in as much as he just didn't drop his arm when she stepped to leave. He followed her, and I had a feeling that was the absolute core of their relationship in one move.

She sighed again, but this one was happier and more content.

"This is new for me. I have never told anyone this. I'm sorry, Caper, but I wanted so badly to have lived the life I told you about in my childhood. It was all a lie, though."

"Even the part about your dad?"

"The part about the giggling flame is not a lie. He did do that, and he wasn't supposed to. We lived in a compound because we were part of a cult, one I escaped. When I left, I decided to rewrite my own history because I never wanted to face what I'd been taught, what I knew was wrong from the time I was too young to understand all the rules, but I still knew they were wrong."

"Are you saying Rick was a part of that cult, too, and that he left but they told everyone he died?" See, those dots were coalescing into a picture I didn't understand, much like the puzzle that had put itself together on the library table. What did it all mean?

"Exactly. And then we never saw him or his wife again. They said it was a tragic accident, but also a penance for the things he was doing that were forbidden, like questioning the leader and having a different opinion than the one handed to us. I was still young when he was there and didn't know that things were any different anywhere else. When you grow up in a cult, you think whatever they do is normal, but there was a small part of me that just couldn't completely fall in line with all the things they wanted us to believe."

"Your dad did that, I bet," Aunt Hellen said.

"I think he did. He stayed for as long as my mom was around. But when she passed away from a horrible infection that she wouldn't go get seen for, he took me away, and then left me with my grandparents and never came back. From thirteen on, I tried to stay in line for them, but I couldn't do it. I started getting in trouble and making bad decisions left and right. I barely knew how to read, so I had tutors and people helping me, but my mom had just died, and my dad had left me, and I didn't know the rules of the real world. So, I rebelled against absolutely everything, no holds barred. If you could do it wrong, I did it wronger. I paid the consequences for a lot of those mistakes and made peace with some of the others over the years, but I've never seen or spoken to anyone from that part of my life again. Until just now."

So much to process, and I wasn't sure where to start with asking for clarification. I could see that this was taking a toll on her, and I felt bad for not just leaving it alone, but there had to be something here that connected those dots.

"Where was this cult headquartered? Are they still operating?" I asked.

"About two hours from here. I have no idea if they still exist or not. Like I said, I left, and that was it, or at least I thought that was it."

"You said Rick had a wife. What was her name?"

"Aspen."

To say that knocked me back a step would have been a very brash understatement. "And what was his name while he was in the cult?"

"Douglas."

Well, dang it. I had hoped that maybe it was Cypress since we were still looking for that, but at least it gave me another piece for the murder board, once I got the time to actually put it up.

"Another tree," I said. "Interesting."

"We all had some sort of tree or plant name. And I very much doubt that Rick, as you call him, had that favor to ask with leaving the dog with you for longer. I think he saw me and got triggered to call me by my name, then flipped the switch quickly so he could leave before I said anything."

"And that could explain why he ran." I paced left and right for about five seconds, then stopped. "Maybe he didn't want you to be able to tell anyone you saw him? He might not know that you ever left the cult, since it would have been after he did."

She shrugged, and Caper moved with her, causing her to laugh softly again. "I think I have a shadow."

"I think you might benefit from an additional shadow," Aunt Hellen said with a smile. "But tell me more about the cult. What did they believe? What was the main core of the mission they were fighting?"

Aunt Hellen had extensive knowledge of cult followings. It was actually what she went to college for, and what she'd been teaching at the local university, until I lured her into early retirement to help me out at the inn.

"I honestly don't know a lot about it. The age to swear fealty and be given the token of the tattoo below the ear wasn't until you were sixteen, and I left before that was going to happen. I know things that were expected on the daily, from being raised there, but you were not allowed to know the secrets of the commitment until it was time. It was like an initiation kind of thing."

"Was your dad the only one with the ability to make candles giggle?" I asked.

"It's funny you ask because my one understanding was that they were looking for someone who could do any kind of out of the ordinary thing, but my dad never showed anyone what he could do, and especially not after my mother yelled at him for playing with fire, then lied about the why when someone came over to check what had happened."

"Would you know Aspen if I showed you a picture of her?" I put my hand up. "No, don't worry about answering because there are no pictures of her, and I'm pretty sure you don't want to go to the morgue to identify her."

"Oh, that's sad." Willow choked up for a second and then seemed to come back into control. "Sorry, to me she's been dead for years, but seeing Rick gave me just a tiny bit of hope I didn't realize had lodged in my head, wishing she might still be someone I could talk to. She was always on the fringe with my dad. Is she the person who died that the chief is trying to blame on you?"

The chief. "Out of curiosity, and you might not know this either, but what was the reason that they were looking for someone who could make flames dance?"

"Well, because long ago they'd had the ability, but something or someone had stripped them of it for something they did. They wanted the ability to either get the magic back or to take it from everyone who had not been punished."

Well, then.

"And what was your dad's name?"

"Cypress."

Chapter 21

Getting the board into the set of rooms I used to live in wasn't an issue. However, getting the thing to stand up and hold all the notes I'd been writing, and pictures I'd been printing, was proving to be a little beyond me. The other times I'd used it, I'd just set it against the wall and called it done. But this case felt much bigger and had far more information than I'd ever had before.

A cult. A cult that was close enough to us to do a quick day trip. One that had lost two members years ago, who had married and both changed their names, and now one of them was dead. And another, whom I suspected might be a member, or at least related to a member, was heading our police department and out for my blood.

Scary was an understatement.

There were stacks of information still behind me, things that needed more information to make them make sense. Like the loan that Emma had applied for and received for her shop. Had it been in her name? Had she been able to secure a co-signer, and that's how she got a loan with little or no history of her before a decade ago? Was whoever had helped her also part of the cult? Had that person been an escapee, too, and were these people all hiding in plain sight together to keep themselves separate from that world?

In other murders, I had certainly looked into things from the deceased person's past, but this felt like so much more than usual.

I wouldn't lie, this whole thing was pretty bizarre, but when I thought more about it, it really wasn't that hard to believe. People did cruel and harmful things. There were rules and codes within the hierarchy here that had to be followed. If someone in that family had done a truly bad thing and had been stripped of their powers, then it made sense to punish them to the full extent, even if it meant their powers were kept from those down the lineage. I just hadn't been aware there was a War of the Worlds going on, and now that I did know, I kind of wished that I had been kept in the dark.

But even with this war brewing, why kill Emma? Had someone from that world finally found her when she'd gone into hiding over a decade ago and had killed her for defiling the cult and leaving them?

Or had Rick killed Emma, originally thinking he'd play it off as a wounded widower? So many of those true crime podcasts always started and ended with the husband for a reason. But when he'd seen Willow, he ran. Just in case he thought they might take his life if they knew where he was?

And how did the chocolates fit into this whole thing? And someone taking Mrs. Lincoln's dog? And a door that Earl couldn't get into, one that I couldn't swear had been there over the years I'd gone into the basement? What about the overly cryptic messages I'd been receiving from the books? And the puzzle? The burning note on the pool table?

So many questions. Ones that I was furiously scribbling down in my notebook, so once I had everyone here and spilling the tea they'd been brewing, those answers could go up on the board, too.

I just needed something, one thing, to make the whole thing snap together like the puzzle had done piece by piece in the library.

Speaking of that, I hadn't yet explained the tree picture to anyone. Really, I hadn't done anything more than ask everyone to let everyone else who wasn't there with us in the lobby know dinner was on its way in, and I had some info that I needed to run by everyone. It was the only way I knew how to do this.

I hadn't let Poobah know I thought I had found Cypress just yet, either. I was reluctant to ask Willow to let me look for her dad without exploring more information about what we already had. Part of me was irritated with myself for not just jumping the gun and finding this Cypress to demand any answers he might have, and why he'd show up as a tree on my puzzle. But the other part of me did not want to go charging in with no real foundation of what I needed from him. I didn't want to ruin my one chance to talk with him, if that was all he gave us.

And so here I was, leaning the board against the wall in the room and using pushpins, tape, and even some adhesive putty that I made from a recipe Glennis had in the kitchen for easy, everyday solutions for the DIY inclined. I trusted myself far more with cornstarch, water, and white vinegar than I ever would have with trying to put a chicken in the oven.

While I had been in the kitchen, I'd tried to get the old cookbook to talk to me again, since I'd never gotten the message when Willow had first come. But nothing happened. No matter what question I asked, or how many times I asked it.

Frustrated to the core, I'd come back to the rooms and got down to the business of organizing things. We'd eat first, and then reconvene here to go over anything we had come up with.

It sounded silly, and really it was, because who was I to think I could solve a murder that the police couldn't? Yes, it had worked out the other two times, but this time my life and reputation were the ones at stake, and I definitely was not a fan of that change.

But I had to believe this, too, would work out in the end, as it had the other two times. I had no idea how or when, but I sent a quick request to the universe that it would be simple and quick.

Right at six, people came streaming into the dining room from all directions. Caper and his family, along with Daffy, came through the French doors leading out into the backyard, where the cottage sat. My parents strolled in with Anjanetta and Clive, her husband. Mena came in hot on their heels by herself, since I had specifically asked that she not bring Micah. We needed to be able to speak freely about everything. We couldn't do that with people in the room who didn't have some knowledge of the talents we were discussing. Once we organized everything and got some more earthly concrete answers, Micah would be the first one I called, followed closely by Norm, but not just yet.

Dean and Poobah came in last, Moose and Taboo, the unlikely duo hanging around with each other, and immediately going to Daffy so she also could be included in their animal circle.

As I looked out across the room, it was interesting to think about where I was a little over a year ago. I'd had friends and family, acquaintances, too. I was never lonely, but I was often alone, doing my job, staying as the anchor for all the people in my life who were out and about, but always knew this was home base.

And now, I had a husband, an extended family, my own family all here under one roof, and to say I was blessed was also an understatement.

Now I just had to keep myself out of jail to enjoy the fruits of all these journeys.

Poobah and Dean delivered the strombolis to the center of the table and doled out the paper plates and plasticware. Yes, we could have done regular dishes and silverware, but I didn't want to be responsible for dishes tonight, and I had a feeling no one else did either.

"Dig into dinner and then we're going to dig into all that's been happening around here."

They took me at my word as the strombolis were divided up and passed around. There was a light here at this table that the human eye wouldn't be able to see, but I'd have bet my last book anyone who stumbled upon us all would be able to feel the vibe of community and togetherness, and that was just as good.

Jokes ran rampant around the table, and I couldn't miss the way Caper and Willow smiled at each other. I did wonder if things were going to work out for the little family in the cottage this time and hoped they would. They were happy right now, and that was enough. I didn't need answers to everything right away, though, believe me, I would have liked them regardless.

Finally, dinner was done, and I shepherded everyone into the situation room. I didn't know what else to call it, and I didn't share the name aloud with anyone. Though I had to stop myself from making a sign and posting it on the door to cover the word "Private" that remained from when these had been my rooms.

I'd moved a couple of the chairs from the hallway into the room and had asked Isaac and Amelia to bring a couple more from the dining room after we were done eating. Everyone should be comfortable because we might be here for a little bit. Or it could be quick if no one had managed to find anything new. That was an option I did not want to entertain until I absolutely had to.

Once the room was filled with all the family, I stood up at the board, feeling a little bit like I was trying to start a pyramid scheme and really wanted you to toss me money so you could sell my new life-changing serum.

I glanced over at Dean, who gave me a thumbs-up. Heaven help me. The sea of faces was so much more than I was used to. The first time, it had mainly been Dean and me, because his life was on the line. Then Mena joined in the second time because her life had been on the line. The third time, I was trying to protect Glennis, though she had not wanted me to.

But this time, I was center stage in a number of ways and found myself far more uncomfortable doing this in front of everyone. I released a quiet breath and told myself to pull my big girl panties up. My life was as important as the other three, and this could hurt all of us, not just me, if we didn't figure out what was going on in our little town.

Okay, then, let's rock.

"We have a lot of questions, but not a ton of answers. I'm hoping you all can fill in some of the holes in this board." I gestured as if I were Vanna White, and there was a snicker behind me. It could have been Anjanetta or Mena, or quite possibly both. And for some reason, it made me realize that while this chief was out to get me, I had a ton of people on my side who would make that nearly impossible. I could take it to completely impossible if I made sure the real killer was caught.

"Look, we have a lot of questions and a lot of information, but none of it seems to do anything but bring up more questions. We need a thread to pull. Anyone have anything that they bring new to the table? Or the board, as the case may be. We need someone to spill the tea. Who's it going to be?"

Isaac squirmed in his chair. Mena checked her phone. Willow looked off into the distance. Poobah ran his thumb over the top of his walking stick. Dean shrugged his shoulders, and the rest of the room just stared at me.

"Anything? We had so many starts with the dog being stolen and the door being locked behind me, the chocolates, and now Rick, but we don't have anything on any of it?" I in no way meant to sound accusatory. I was just disappointed. The books had sparkled, the words had come, even if they didn't totally make sense, since they weren't sentences or even full thoughts. They were just individual words. I stood back from the board and tried to see any points that were almost built out instead of only being an idea without any substance.

And my eye landed on the puzzle info I'd reluctantly put up there, but hadn't made a big deal of. Willow was happy here and happy with reconnecting with the only family that mattered. I did not want to drag her out into the open and make her deal with an absent father just to prove something wasn't true that I knew without a shadow of a doubt wasn't true. I hadn't killed Emma, and there was nothing the chief could make happen that would prove something that wasn't true. It just couldn't happen.

Willow rose from her chair and came to the board. "I've been thinking about this for the last hour, and I wish I had asked when we were actually in the conversation, but now's as good a time as any. Why did you ask for my father's name? I didn't get the feeling it was just mild curiosity, especially when you asked about everyone having names having to do with plants and trees. When I told you, there was a pause, and then you moved us right along to the next thing and told us you'd see us at dinner. There had to be significance there, or I have the feeling you wouldn't have moved us along and out the door." She waved a hand over the board, and the pages fluttered like a gentle breeze had entered the room to swirl in a lazy dance.

"I don't know if you want to do this," I said the words and had never meant them more.

"If, for some reason, my father killed someone he had been in the cult with, and he's responsible for a person dying, then I have nothing but anger about it and him. He left me decades ago, Roxy. I'm not going to be sad if the only place I ever see him is behind bars."

"Are you sure? You were struck pretty hard when I told you Emma was dead, and you hadn't seen her in years."

"That was because seeing Douglas, even just for a moment, took me back to other times, especially since we had just been talking about the flickering candles my father used to make me smile in the middle of things going wrong. I don't know if I would have felt the same if I had happened upon her at the counter of her flower shop."

Poobah tapped his walking stick on the floor and then walked over to join us at the board. "What is your father's name?"

"I told Roxy it was Cypress. Everyone had to have a name that had to do with the forest or a garden center. Emma had taken the name Aspen when she was originally brought into the fold as a very young girl. I don't know what her first name was, but it had been lost in the years between. Douglas is for Douglas fir. I was born Willow because my parents were already in the cult when I was born. My father had been Jeff before he and my mom got together, and once they were married, he took the name Cypress. Your eyes went wide when I said it, Roxy, but then you shooed us out and never told me why."

"Roxanne..." Poobah dragged out the last syllable of my name. I guess I could just be thankful he didn't use my middle name.

"Before we get into that, and I promise we will," I said to the room in general, but I was looking at Willow, "let me give you a snapshot of what we're dealing with. Maybe that way it will make more sense or trigger something you heard, but didn't seem significant at the time, and so you didn't mention it."

I stepped back over to the board while Willow resumed her seat next to Caper. I could do this.

But first, I wiped my palms on the hips of my skirt and prepared to take the plunge. I only hoped I wasn't about to make things worse.

Chapter 22

"Why is that significant, Roxanne Elizabeth?" my mother asked with some steel in her voice as she looked at me. Uh oh.

It occurred to me I'd been collecting things, but had not been sharing them with everyone. To be fair, a lot had been going on, and I couldn't text everyone every time something happened or nothing would happen, because I'd be stuck on my phone.

I should have started tonight with a rundown of everything I had. Doing it this way, by trying to get info without thinking to give any except for assignments, hadn't been my best idea. I was left holding the bag on this one because I had only told people what I thought they needed to know in order for them to get back to me with what I was looking for. Oops.

I could rectify that now, though, and I'd better do it quickly before my mom puts me on restriction.

"Let me explain."

"Please, go ahead and explain yourself," Anjanetta said. Great, all I needed was for Mena to chime in with her own snarky comments, and it would be four against one.

But when I looked at my younger sister, all she did was wave me on.

"I'm trying to think about how to make all the info make sense. I wish I had more to give you, but I've got lots of little things that don't appear to be connected. But I can't just call them coincidences because that just isn't possible."

Where to start? From the look on Willow and Poobah's faces, I decided to start there.

"I was looking for something to help me through the bibliomancy, so I went to the library, as a bibliomancer does, and books started glowing, a bunch of them, and so did the puzzle closet." I ran them through the words I'd stuck to the board behind me. "Green. Crowded. Beware. Fortune. Creature. Dating. Happy. Ruin. Light. Justice. Close. Marriage. Renewal. Secrets." I poked at the paper, like messing with it might give me the answers I so craved. "None of it made sense. Then we opened the puzzle box, the one with the Ferris Wheel on it, but it started putting itself together on the table, and it was a picture that in no way could have been created by those pieces. And yet when it was done, it was a stunning watercolor with three trees—an aspen, a willow, and a cypress. Poobah had made the connection with someone he and Duchy had been brought to cleanse many years ago, and Poobah speculated that Aspen was Emma, which Willow has confirmed. We knew Willow, but didn't know who Cypress would be. Until I talked with you earlier," I told Willow. "I didn't want to alarm you, and I didn't want to make you have to go back through that time when your father left. I thought I'd see if we could get any additional info so we wouldn't have to do what I don't want to make you do."

"Convoluted, but understood," my sister-in-law said. "I would tell you that you just had to ask. But since we just met, I can't expect you to understand I would always rather face things head-on and grab them by the horns than ignore them and hope I never get picked up and thrown into the arena."

"Nicely said, Mom." Amelia gave her a few claps, and the tension in the room seemed to dissipate in a flash. That child. She was a wonder.

"Thank you, honey."

"You never say things like that to me," Caper said.

Amelia snickered. "If you'd be profound like Mom, I promise to notice. Normally, though, I'm usually trying to get you to at least give me full sentences, not grunts. I also can't want them to make sense in a deep metaphorical way."

Oh, ow! But Caper was the first one to laugh, which let the rest of us all do the same thing.

"Touché." He bowed his head to her.

"Nicely said, Dad."

Which sent another round of laughter. With how heavy things had gotten recently, I had a feeling we all needed this quick reprieve before we got into the nitty-gritty.

"So, my father's name is the same as the one tree in the picture," Willow said, getting us back on track. "And Aspen would have been past, I would be present, and Cypress would be future. Were you told the immediate future?" She gripped her hands in her lap, and Caper reached over to cover them with his own hand.

"If there were a way around this, I'm sure Roxy would have come up with anything and everything before bringing it here." He gave her a squeeze, and she squeezed back.

So very true. "We don't have to do this tonight, obviously. I truly believe we need to fill as many of these holes as we can before we even approach him. Going in with a half-cocked gun and no ammo is not going to be our best bet. We want to be prepared, and the only way we're going to do that is to have as much info as possible so we ask the right questions if we can find him."

Isaac started squirming on his chair again, and his computer on his lap tipped to the one side. Dean caught it before it could crash to the floor, then rolled his eyes when he looked at the screen.

"Really?" he said, addressing his nephew.

"I couldn't help myself."

"Of course, you couldn't." Dean turned the screen so that everyone could see it. There on the screen was a blog site for a man named Jeffery Cypress, an accountant in good standing in the small town of Hillsboro, about two hours from here. The face was similar to Willow's, the eyes were the same, the smile was an echo of the one I was looking at, and the hair was exactly the same color.

She didn't gasp or choke up. She simply came closer and then used Isaac's mousepad on the laptop to scroll through the site. "This would be him. He had done the budgeting and the intake at the compound. I used to count pennies with him and roll all our change because we didn't want to send it through a coin machine at a business. They took a percentage that the leader did not think was theirs to take. Rolling meant we got every cent that we had taken in."

"How did they make money?" Poobah asked. "We were approached many years ago by Emma's father to cleanse her of her iniquities, but then we never heard from them again. They were both well-dressed, and she appeared to be well-taken care of, or we would have been more concerned for her welfare."

"I'm not entirely sure. I was young, so not involved in a lot of what they did. But I remember a lot of people going to street fairs with these charm-type things they said could cure anything or make your dreams come true. The cops came once when something bad happened to a person they sold something to, so maybe they were also available for people who were looking to poison or hurt another person?"

Things snapped together in my brain—not everything, but maybe a thing or two.

"Were they ever in the business of making chocolates?"

"Yes, I can't stand the stuff. The air was always scented with that smell, and it made me sick to my stomach. I know other people love it, but yuck."

I glanced at my mother, and then we both looked at Mena. It didn't take talent necessarily to curse things. Or perhaps in taking the talents away from the line, the higher-ups had opened a door they had not anticipated. I did not like the idea of magic being used to kill. But if Emma had also eaten any of the chocolates out of the other box that was found at the flower shop, and had no one to save her, except Taboo, who had been on the other side of the refrigerator glass door, then we might be dealing with something far beyond anything I had ever imagined.

"Chocolates were here in the house at my rehearsal, and Mena passed out after eating one." I tapped my finger to the board where I'd put a picture of chocolates surrounded by words about what had happened, what my mom had done, and then what she thought caused everything. It wasn't the exact box and didn't have the symbol on it that Poobah had recognized. That was another picture on the board. I unstuck it from its position next to a few paragraphs about the burning piece of paper on the pool table, and the way the books had lit up like Christmas in the library, but only offered single words, not sentences, to at least kind of guide me to what I was supposed to be doing.

I took the picture of the symbol in Duchy's journal and held it out for Willow to take. She wrapped her arms around her middle and bit her bottom lip. After a quick glance, she shut her eyes and choked.

"I'm sorry," I said quickly, yanking the picture behind my back. "I'm sorry, I took it away. I didn't know that would be your reaction, or I wouldn't have done it."

With her eyes open again, she reached out to grip my arm. "No, no, please don't apologize. It's important, and I can do this. I had no idea how much I had shoved down inside me to survive. And if nothing else, this is at least a safe place to pull some of those memories out and deal with them for the first time ever."

Caper chose that moment to place a hand over hers on my arm. "You're not alone. You've never been alone, but here, there's literally no place you can go that won't have someone waiting or something happening. Welcome back."

Her smile was shy, and she touched her lips with two fingers, then touched those two fingers to his mouth.

"Thank you. I can do this." She shook out her light hair, shoved her shoulders back, and took in a deep breath. "Okay, show me again," she said with only a slight quiver in her words.

"If you're sure?" I said.

"Yes, absolutely sure. Do it now."

My mom moved from where she'd been sitting on the couch next to my dad and stood on the other side of Willow from Caper. She put a hand on her shoulder and nodded for Caper to do the same on his side. I couldn't hear the words she was chanting under her breath, but the way her mouth was moving was enough to let me know that there was some serious protection going on right now, and I was never so grateful in my life.

I brought the picture out slowly, allowing Willow time to decide she just couldn't face it yet. But she was a strong one and never even blinked as I fully presented the paper on the palms of both of my hands. She didn't touch it, and I hadn't expected her to, but she did take in the whole thing at once at first, then started roving her eyes over the different pieces of the symbol. She traced the knot in the middle in one slow motion and then followed the outlining lines that created a kind of crest.

"Yes, that's the exact thing that everyone has on them in some place and in some way. I had heard that, at one time, they used a branding iron before they began moving into tattooing. That symbol and several others were the absolute heart of the group. It means protection to those who believe and possible death to those who don't."

"But Duchy didn't pass for several years after seeing the symbol," I put in. "How was she protected?"

"For one, I'm sure she would have protected herself, dear." Poobah went to the picture and studied it again, looking at it left and right. "And my guess is because she only saw it, and didn't consume anything it was on, was her saving grace. The man had a box of chocolates with him at the time and offered them to us in payment, but Duchy told him she was allergic, and then we didn't speak of it again. Obviously, I can't ask her why she did that, and if she knew, it might have been an issue, but he had looked reluctant to hand them over at all. It was only after Aspen, who was eventually Emma, prompted him to remember he'd been given a gift to pass on to the person who could cleanse her that he brought them out of his overcoat. His grip on the box, now that I think about it, was incredibly strong, to the point that the edges he was gripping were crumbling under his fingertips."

"So, he didn't want to hand them over. He had been given them just in case you called him out, or refused, and maybe brought in the authorities?"

"Aspen's father brought her to you to have her cleansed?" Willow asked, getting out of her chair to pace.

"Yes, when she was a teenager."

Biting her lip, Willow paced back and forth in front of her husband until he gently grasped her hand and pulled her to a slow stop.

"You don't have to be the only one to figure this out, love. We're all here for the same purpose. Spit it out, whatever you're thinking, and let us workshop it."

"We're not planning a heist, love. We're solving one."

His smile was radiant. "And it's so much better to be thwarting the bad guys instead of trying to outthink anyone who was trying to make the same heist work."

Finally, she really smiled and sat on his lap sideways. His arm braced her back, and she touched his forehead with hers. "It could be for money. If this chief wants to ruin the talented, as Roxy says, then it is possible they needed a victim to be able to pull Roxy into the murder, someone they knew she was going to see. Somewhere, they knew she was going to be. Emma's husband was supposedly stuck at a campground, right? He called the wedding planner to let her know Roxy needed to pick up the flowers. But what if he was still in the area? Perhaps to make sure he was there to lock the door, knowing he could still make it to the campground before the cops were called after Roxy found Emma in the refrigerator. There's nothing to say he didn't also call that chief, too, and let him know it was done, and that Roxy was on her way there."

"But why would he kill his own wife? I thought they were pretty happy together." I had never seen them argue, and anytime I asked Emma how things were going, she always had a glowing report and praise for Rick and his part in the shop.

"When they were declared dead, the story was that Aspen wanted out and she dragged her husband with her unwillingly," Willow answered. "He didn't want to leave, but he did because he loved her, but always thought he could bring her back after she got a taste of the real outside world. When they were killed, the group put it down to a strike from above for even attempting to leave and used it as an example of what could happen if you broke your loyalty there."

"Jeez, that is intense." Even the council of our group knew that if someone wanted to go, they were able to and still keep their contacts, their family, but chose to take a different path. There was no shame in that, no guilt in choosing one over the other. This cult thing was a whole different animal.

"Do you think the chief paid Rick to kill his wife, or do we think that he already wanted to do it, and this was a way to literally, and metaphorically, kill two birds with one stone?" Dean asked.

"Cypress is wondering when you want to meet, and if tomorrow is okay at the café on the square. The one right next to the flower shop, by the way. He knows the owner since he does her taxes." Isaac had been quietly clicking away on his laptop this whole time. I should have been braced for him to pop out with a plan, though.

"Who does he want to meet?" I asked.

"You, of course, Roxy, since the buzz in the rumor mill is that you might be on the right track to catching the actual killer and thwarting that jerk who's top cop right now."

Did I want to get in the middle of some kind of feud between warring cultists and ex-cultists? I didn't really have a choice at this point.

Chapter 23

"I'm not sure I like this," Amelia said when she found me at the front desk the next morning. We'd all gone to bed with heads full of info, but still some missing pieces.

"It will be fine. I have protectors that will go with me just in case."

"I could send a windstorm in there if anything bad starts to happen."

I kissed her on the forehead.

"I could. I've been practicing."

"I know you have been, but let's not take it out on the road for a little longer. I want to keep the talent use to a minimum right now. I'm just there to talk and get some more information. I don't want to mix things up just yet. But I'll keep you in mind, promise."

Mom and Dad came down the stairs, talking quietly between themselves. I knew they were concerned, but I also knew that they had not been around for my last three investigations. I wasn't as much of a newbie as they probably thought I was. I had things in place and contingency plans like no one's business.

"What are you two up to today?" I asked as they came into the lobby.

"Well, we were hoping that this adorable lady would consider going on the ferry with us and show us things we haven't seen in a long time."

"Basically, you're going to get me out of the way so that I don't get hurt in case something goes sideways," Amelia said matter-of-factly, no angst or upset in her tone. "I approve. Let me go get my backpack, and tell Dad that I'll be out of his thinning hair. Don't leave without me, Didi and Bopper."

I muffled my giggle as she skipped out of the lobby, through the dining room, and slammed the French doors behind her on her way out to the cottage. Didi and Bopper stood there looking shellshocked. I couldn't blame them. Several parts of her response could be the thing that put those looks on their faces, but it could also be everything combined into one adorable ball of energy that was our darling Amelia.

"Didi," Mom said with a smile.

"And Bopper?" Dad said with a quirked eyebrow.

They both had huge smiles on their faces, so I just nodded.

"I like it." Mom straightened her light jacket on her shoulders and struck a pose like she was about to do a runway. "Didi. I was so hoping that would be the one she chose."

"According to Isaac, she had already considered several options, Dad. She was originally going to call you Queenie, per Isaac, but they didn't have anything to match it that didn't sound odd for Dad."

"Bopper?" This from Dad, who looked a little confused, but also pleased.

"My inside info is that she was going through a bunch of research in hopes she was allowed to call you by a grandparent name, but none of the usual stuff was sitting right with her. Because there's Poobah and we had Duchy, it needed some pizzazz, and you both needed something that wasn't common. Boppa is what came up most, but then the story of you dancing all the time in the kitchen came up, and you became Bopper to Mom's Didi, which is her first name twice in short."

"That's a very thought-out and researched kind of thing to do." He sounded impressed, as he should.

"Seriously, neither of those kids does anything halfway. But be careful with her, she's still a little sneaky when it comes to certain things. She grew up with different rules, and too fast in some areas. If she says something you want to push back on, instead, ask her why she thinks that. Her answers can be hard to stomach because she's so innocent in giving them, but the overall concept is rarely that innocent. It's just how she grew up."

"We had our own set of mischief-makers, if I recall, for different reasons, but the same thrust is there for all children, no matter how they grew up. I'm pretty sure we can handle her. Isaac, too, if you think he'd want to come with us," Dad said.

"He's knee-deep in research at the moment and having a blast, so let's let him stay here. Maybe another time you could take them to a museum or dinner."

"I'm thinking something a little farther afield, but we can talk about that later."

Amelia came back into the foyer with her backpack on and a light jacket tied around her waist. "Ready when you are. And, Roxy, I promise not to do anything I shouldn't while we're out. I know the rules." There was that cheeky smile again.

I hugged her and then both of my parents before sending them on their way to the ferry. Dean usually ran it, but this was his wedding week, so he'd taken time off. The other people who stepped in on his vacations knew what to do and how to do it, so they were in good hands.

I watched them drive out of the circle in front and breathed a sigh of relief, because that meant three fewer people here to worry about if something went horribly wrong.

Yes, I'd assured them we were just going to talk, and that I had tons of protection, and that was true to some extent, but in reality, I was also shaking on the inside about how this might go down.

I had my own backpack, and I'd put a few smaller books in there, just in case I needed to use them in my quest for that information. Then I set off for the café down the road, thirty minutes earlier than we had agreed on. I wanted to get the lay of the land, and also hopefully talk with Teresa, the owner, before Cypress, or rather Jeff, got there.

Walking past Petal Paradise made me sad. The whole inside was dark, and there was a sign on the door that said they'd be back eventually. I didn't know when or how with Rick on the run, and possibly the killer, and no Emma to make things bloom, or arrange them into beautiful bouquets once they were ready to be shown off to their best glory.

I shook my head at myself. There were many things that could happen, and perhaps Rick wasn't the actual killer. Maybe he really was on the run because he thought the cult had found him. He could have put two and two together and come up with the cult having killed Emma and was now coming for him next.

That wasn't the way I thought it had gone down, but I could be wrong. I wasn't going to make any real decisions until after I found out why Cypress had shown up on my puzzle, and how this all came together to make a picture of three trees in the same spot, but from different times. Did they serve three different purposes or just three different phases of the same purpose?

I wouldn't know until I started asking questions.

Entering the café, I went to the front counter and was pleased to see that they had my favorite tropical fruit smoothie on the specials board. When it was my turn to order, I was happy to be across from Teresa.

"You must have heard that the smoothie was back," she said with a smile. "I was about to call you, or drop you a note, but I figured you'd find out some way if it was meant to be. Rumors tend to run rampant sometimes in our little town, the good and the bad." One of her eyebrows shot up, and I groaned inside. I hoped with everything I had that she did not think I would have killed her neighbor for any reason.

"Don't I know it." I laughed. "I'm actually here to meet someone about business. There are some things I'd like to let go of over at the inn so I can concentrate on my new husband and running the part of the inn I like best, the guests. Mathing confuses me sometimes, and if I could just hand over a box of receipts to this Jeff guy and have him deal with it all, I would be much happier."

"Jeff is the absolute best. Came highly recommended by Emma. I always take her recommendations. She's spot on every time. Or at least she was." Teresa's eyes started glistening, and I was afraid she was going to bawl her eyes out. I'd rather not be standing here when she did that. I didn't need another assumed black mark on my record in town.

"I took her recommendations, too. Sharon did an amazing job with the wedding."

Those tears dried up pretty quickly. "Now that one I'm not too sure about, but if you say she did a good job, then I might take a second look at her for our soft grand opening of a new section of our shop. I'm finally getting to bring in books. I got all the permits and whatnot for the upstairs to be a bookstore."

This was the first I was hearing of this, and it nearly made me giddy. "Rumors don't travel over to us as often. I didn't even know you were considering that. How exciting!"

"Well, if you're looking to get rid of any of your library, I'm in the market. I'm doing used and new, and we'll have some events in the area upstairs." She seemed to catch herself. "Oh, that's not going to infringe on your business, is it? I hadn't even thought of that. I'm so sorry!"

I put my hand over hers on the counter. "Teresa, seriously, calm down. It's a totally different kind of business, and that's awesome. If you ever want Glennis to help with some of the bigger items that aren't breads and muffins, just give her a call. She's amazing at serving crowds."

"That would be wonderful. I'll check in with you next week sometime then. I was going to have Emma do some arrangements with books in them for prizes at book clubs, but I can't now. It's so sad."

"It is." And since we were back to the topic without tears, I had a question. "Was there anything going on over there that might be gossip or rumor I also hadn't heard? Like I said, I don't always get all the news, since I'm not often out and about around here. I'm going to change that as soon as we open back up now that I've got a permanent helper in Dean."

"And he's quite the homerun, I must say." Teresa was not a day under seventy, so her remarks made my smile even bigger.

"You would have given me a run for my money if you could, huh?"

"Bah, I'm too old for that kind of crap, dear. I would have thought Rick was, too, but to each his own, I guess."

Wait. What? Rick how? Rick why? Rick who? "Rick next door? The Rick who was married to Emma until a few days ago?"

"My, my, my, you really don't get any of the gossip." She crossed her arms on the counter and leaned in, so I did the same.

What on earth was I about to learn, and why didn't I have my notebook out to capture it?

"So, for a little backstory, long ago this was a single house, and then someone wanted some more money and made it into a double. But they only wanted to get more money, not shovel more out, which meant they went a little shoddy on how they separated the two sides. It happened at a house I owned before. My word, having to listen to twenty-four hours a day of someone playing those shoot 'em up games was enough to make a lady crazy. But I digress."

She leaned in more, but I stayed where I was this time because I didn't want to bump noses with her.

"Anyway, I heard that you are being slammed as the murderer, and I just can't believe it—even though you've found three other bodies and that alone should be strange—but I just can't believe you'd do something like that, not even once, much less four times. I mean, come on! You're not Dexter. Am I right?"

I used all of my physical powers not to back away from her, but wow, that was a punch in the gut. Especially because if she was saying it now, I was certain I was not the first person she'd shared those thoughts with. She'd probably told her whole coffee klatch by now, and maybe even the chamber of commerce.

Yikes.

"Of course, you're right. All three happened in or around the inn. If I hadn't found them, someone else would have."

"See, that's what I told Martha down at the pharmacy the other day when I was in there picking up my prescriptions. Gerald, at the coin-op, was there, and he agreed, too. We know who you are, and we're letting anyone and everyone who has a bad word about you know."

This time, I used all my physical strength not to roll my eyes. At this point, I had to admit everyone in town had some sort of opinion, and I could only hope most of them believed I couldn't and wouldn't do this.

"I'm digressing again! Lady, you need to keep me on track, or I'll be off and running, telling you about how that planner lady doesn't seem to be able to get her dates right. Anyway, the builders didn't do the best job with the back walls of this place, and I can't swear by it, but I would bet my next scone delivery on the fact there was often a third person in the store, but only when Emma wasn't there, if you get my drift. And that person might just have had a very feminine voice, if you know what I mean. And they weren't always talking..." She trailed off and gave me a squinty-eyed look like I wasn't catching on quickly enough.

The fact was, I knew precisely what she was talking about, but I'd also just seen Cypress—Jeff—walk in the door, and I had wanted to already be seated and ready to rule the table when he got here.

However, this could be very important, so I stuck it out at the counter. "Any idea who that other woman might be that Rick was messing around with? Because that could be super helpful."

"And you know how I love to be super helpful."

"Yes, I'm very aware of your super helpfulness." I smiled, as I also kept track of Cypress standing four deep behind me, waiting to order something. I could still get back to the table before he did if I moved things along here and didn't make him take a seat until the line died down.

"Anyway, I just thought that was information you might want to take a gander at. Emma was a good woman, but she came from a rough background. Told me once that she was on the run. I asked why she decided to settle down then, and she said that someone here had done her a solid when she was a teenager, so she thought this was the safest place if she ever got in trouble again. I guess that didn't exactly work out for her, now did it?"

Sadly, no, I thought. But I also knew I could at least bring her killer to justice, just as soon as I got through this conversation with Cypress.

"I don't want to keep your line waiting. Thanks for the lowdown, and I'll let you know if I think of any other questions. You've been very helpful."

"I aim to please, well, not everyone, but definitely you. I have some business over your way tomorrow. I'll stop by because I have an idea I want to run by you."

"I'll look forward to it."

And I would because that meant that hopefully I could get through all this and be normal by tomorrow. Or not exactly normal, since my normal involved being able to do magic and get books to tell me secrets even the author didn't know, but that was for another day, hopefully one where I wasn't a suspect.

Now, I watched covertly as Cypress shuffled his way to the counter behind the other three people in front of him. He was tall. His hair was white, and his shoulders were narrow. I imagined him being able to make flames dance and giggle for his young daughter, hoping to brighten her life, and then having to leave her in the care of his own parents in an effort to save her. But then why didn't he try to come back into her world once he'd set himself up as a reputable accountant? He had grandchildren who would have probably already had a cool name picked out for him if he had just reached out at any time.

Although, when Willow was in jail, would he have felt it was inappropriate to try to see her at such a low point in her life? Did he think maybe getting involved with her could put his own career and the new life he's made at risk? I could see both points. It would be better to go in with an open mind to this conversation instead of already having an opinion and then bouncing anything he said off of that opinion.

Talk about complicated. He glanced behind him and zeroed in on me, and then seemed to be startled to see me at the table. Because he'd seen me before when he'd locked the door behind me after murdering Emma? Or because he hadn't thought I'd shown up yet? I'd had Isaac tell him what I would be wearing, and I'd stuck to the red shirt with a black flower pin right below my shoulder. I thought the flower was fitting since Emma had loved her flowers.

I sent him a small wave, and he nodded, then turned back around to place his order. Since someone in the back would bring out my smoothie when it was ready, I settled into my seat, took out the folder from my backpack, and got ready to do some serious interrogating. I had a list of questions I was determined to ask, and another to pick a couple to throw in there if time and his personality allowed.

Ready to rumble, that was me.

Unfortunately, when I looked up from my notes, Cypress was nowhere to be found, and the shop door banged closed behind me.

Chapter 24

Suppressing the absolute urge to scream to the high heavens was almost insurmountable, but I did it, just barely.

When I looked out the windows that fronted the café, it was to find Clarence from the butcher shop walking slowly down the sidewalk. No way could Cypress have left the café and been completely out of sight in that time. So, did that mean he was still in here somewhere?

I rose from the table and approached the empty counter. "Hey there, did Jeff say why he left without meeting with me?"

Teresa looked around. "He didn't say much, just put his order in, but he'll be back for it, I'm sure. If you want someone who's more of a talker, you might want to look at Dolly over at the tax prep. She's got really good ways of doing things and is for less complicated kinds of businesses, you know what I mean?"

I didn't, but I wasn't going to get sucked into that conversation with her because I really needed to know where Cypress had gone. I could deal with the embarrassment of the local tax preparer needing a jolt of caffeine to deal with my recordkeeping later.

"So where did he go?"

"In the back, like he always does on the days he comes in, to make sure my inventory matches up with my computer. Thinking more about it, Dolly probably wouldn't be able to handle everything you've got going on at the inn. I highly recommend Jeff. He always goes that one step beyond."

"Can I see if I can catch him before he gets too engrossed? I promise not to touch anything else. You can have my smoothie delivered back there when it's ready, if that's not too inconvenient."

She shrugged. "Not inconvenient at all, especially since it's right here, ready for you. Just take it now."

Even better. Then I wouldn't have to worry about being interrupted during our conversation, and we could be out of the middle of a room that was filling up this morning, as it always did. Of course, I'd miss out on being surrounded by enough people that Cypress wouldn't try to harm me, but he sounded safe, and I was going to go with my gut on this one.

I stayed close to the wall as I went through the bakery and kitchen, then found the hallway that was set up like a shotgun house. Every room had a door to the left, and the wall to the right would have been the one that was connected to Petal Paradise. Because that space was closed now, I wasn't surprised that I heard nothing from next door.

Each door on the left was ajar, so I peeked into every one before finally coming to the office in the very back, right before the exit out into the alley behind the building.

And there was Cypress with his head bent over the stacks of papers in front of him. He looked like a professor grading papers with a red pen, and I wondered if Teresa wasn't quite as good as she thought she was. That was probably confirmed when he lifted his head, rolled his eyes, and groaned as he smacked the pen down on the desk. "Just once!" he said.

I leaned on the frame of the door and waited for him to notice me. First, he clamped a hand onto his forehead, then slid his hand down over his face, pulling down and stretching his skin.

Finally, he groaned and shook his head. "Nothing for it but to dive in," he said.

"I can give you a quick break from the tedium of trying to figure out what exactly Teresa thinks is an expense and what is a loss, if you wouldn't mind having that meeting we agreed to online."

He shoved back in his rolling chair and careened into the bookcase behind him.

"Sorry, didn't mean to scare you. I thought it would be best to let you get your irritation out before I start asking you some questions."

"Are you a reporter? I don't know anything about the murder of the poor woman next door, so you might want to check back with your original source before you dive into whatever questions you think you have for me." He closed the folder in front of him, stacked other papers on top of it, then tapped it on the desk to align all the edges.

Part of me wanted to come fully into the room, close the door, and start demanding some real conversation and answers. But the way he looked at me kept me from doing it.

"You think I'm a reporter?"

"You're all the same. Make it seem like you just had a random question, and then suddenly, I'm bombarded and misquoted. I'm not having it."

Why would he think I was a reporter? And why was he being chased by them? "But we set up a meeting today. You and I were supposed to meet over drinks here to discuss a few things, including possibly asking you to take on my books." I was not unaware of the possible double duty that last line was going to do, but I powered through when he just stared at me as if he had no idea what I was talking about. "We set up a meeting last night online. You agreed to meet me here. I sent you a rundown of what I'd be wearing, including the black flower pin, so that we wouldn't miss each other."

"No, I never received any kind of communication from you. I was scheduled to be here today because this is the day I always come in to help Teresa with the books. It's a weekly thing."

"Then who was I talking to online?" I left out that it wasn't actually me doing the emailing, but that it was Isaac, because he didn't need to know that.

He shrugged and tapped a finger on his folder. "I have no idea who you were in contact with. It wasn't me, though. Sorry. You might want to check back with whoever sent you the information and see if you can find out who they really are. Now, if you'll excuse me, I have to get back to what I was doing. I get paid hourly and have a commitment this afternoon, so I need to get this done." And he turned back to his folder, opened it up, and took his red pen in hand.

"That can't be right." I was not going to be so easily dismissed. "You're Jeff Cypress, correct? Why did you jump when you looked at me sitting at our table behind you?"

"I am Jeff Cypress, and I didn't jump from seeing you. To be honest, I didn't even notice you were in the room. It was someone whom I thought I recognized from a long time ago, but I dismissed it because it couldn't be possible. He died a long time ago. I went to his funeral."

"There seem to be a lot of should-be-dead people walking around recently. Who was it?"

Avoiding my gaze, he kept his eyes on the folder. "I'd rather not talk about it to someone whose name I don't even know. I have work to do. If you could please pull the door shut behind you when you leave, I'd appreciate it."

That was a clear dismissal, but I still had questions. "Did the man have a name that was a tree? Something like Aspen? Or how about Willow?" Admittedly, that was not a very nice dig, but I needed something here, and I wasn't getting it by keeping my hands clean.

He pinched the bridge of his nose. "Who are you?"

"Roxanne Gleason, now Winchester, and I'm looking into the death of Emma, who was formerly Aspen. A friend of yours, or so I was told by your daughter, Willow, who is right now sitting down the street at my inn, hoping like no other that she could connect with you and introduce her husband and your two grandchildren, if you're willing to step out of the shadows."

I don't know what I had expected him to do. Maybe cry? Or at least tear up? Instead, his head snapped up, and he bared his teeth at me. The gleam in his eye told me violence was only seconds away.

Grabbing my book, all I did was ask it to save me and then opened it up, cracking the spine, which made me shudder, but there was nothing to do for it except hope it flashed with light so hard that he'd be blinded.

I had never thought my talent was one of the important ones, but if it saved me from being attacked, then I promised I would honor it above almost anything else in the world.

Chapter 25

The flash was staggering to me, and it appeared to be worse for Cypress. He shouted, and then slammed his eyes shut and threw his arm up to shield himself from the blinding light. His chair rolled back again with the force of his recoil, and the contents of the bookshelf fell on top of him.

I did indeed slam the door behind me as I left. With everything that had just happened, there was no way I'd be able to walk casually back out into the café and then saunter out the front door, as if things did not feel catastrophic at the moment.

Instead, I chose the back door and yanked the knob so hard I almost tore it off, because I just needed to get out. After fumbling for a second, I realized the door opened out, not in. I shoved this time instead of pulling, and the door opened out to the right. Stepping out as quickly as I could, I carefully closed it behind me, then leaned back against it as I released the breath I'd been holding.

I had to get out of here before he got out from under all the files and chased me down. He knew where I lived, but that wouldn't matter. If I could get there first, I could barricade the thing like a fortress. I would have called the cops, but with Chief Morony at the helm, I doubted he'd do anything to help me.

"Don't you move another muscle." Speaking of Chief Morony...

My gaze darted over the few cars back here in the alley, looking for anyone who could help, but all I found was some random trash rolling along the asphalt and little else. "Do you have a warrant for my arrest? Or perhaps some other legal means of detaining me? I doubt it, and I have way too much to do in order to deal with your ridiculous crap." Spoken with true bravado, even though I was shaking in my flats. We were in the back of a business with no one in sight and I wasn't sure anyone would hear me if I screamed. And even if Jeff did hear me scream, he might be inclined to simply smile and go about his business instead of coming out to see what was going on.

How did I always manage to get myself into these positions? And how on earth was I going to get out of this one? I was very tempted to use the book magic again, but something told me I was not in as imminent danger as I had been with Jeff, and therefore I couldn't count on it to blind him like it had the first man.

"You'll deal with whatever I tell you to deal with."

As ludicrous as it sounded, I stamped my foot on the ground in irritation. "And you have no authority to stop me from walking away. You think you have problems now? Wait until I unleash my real power on you." Of course, there was nothing I could actually unleash, power or otherwise, but if it gave me the brief window I needed to leave, then I was pulling out all the stops.

"Don't you dare!"

What did he think I could do? Hit him with a lightning bolt out of the sky? Throw fire at him at will without a lighter?

"I won't do anything if you let me pass. I get that you think I'm a horrible person, and so is my family, and we took something from you, blah, blah, blah. Blah! But the reality is, I had no idea you even existed, and I still wouldn't know you existed—and I'd be far happier—if it wasn't for the murder of the poor woman next door. Every minute you spend trying to pin this on me is another minute the real killer is getting further away and burying themselves more. How do you know they won't try again because you're so distracted over some family punishment thing that I don't know anything about? How is that working in your favor?"

"I know you did it. There was no one else in the shop, and she was found dead by you."

"That can't be all you have, Moron...y." Whoops, needed to be careful with that. "I have so much information on people not being who they say they are, people doing nefarious things with the numbers, others who've moved in and out of polite society, and others who are impersonating other people, as well as a bunch of people that think other people are dead, but then they find out they are not in no way, shape or form dead. You don't find that interesting? And what about the husband? He has an alibi by being at the campground, but was he? Why did he have a panic attack so bad that they put him in the hospital for observation? Have you checked into him at all? I heard he might have been seeing someone behind Emma's back. So, did he want out of the marriage, but didn't want to lose any of the things they'd built together over the years since leaving their previous situation?"

Why did I suddenly feel like that bad guy at the end, doing the confession monologue about why I killed someone and what clues I thought the person had missed?

"I'm done with you," I said, marching past him. He didn't make a grab for me, so I walked faster. "When I figure out who did this, you'll be the second to know. Maybe ninth. No, definitely fourth. Probably." And then I rounded the corner and made a run for the inn.

I was never so happy that it wasn't very far. As I passed the cop car at the corner, I thought briefly of locking the doors or slashing a tire, but that was beneath me and would probably take too much time, so I skipped it and kept moving down the street.

Running up the stairs to the front door, I pulled my keys out of my pocket just in case it was locked, then literally fell into Dean's arms as he whipped open the door under my hand, pitching me forward.

"Hey, hey, hey. What happened?" he asked, concerned shadowing his voice.

"Just get me in the house, and we'll talk. Close the door. Now."

He did as I asked without any more questions. As soon as I heard the lock click into place, I went directly to the rooms with the murder board. I was missing something, and I would find it. I had to know who had actually done this before Moron took me into custody and then maybe made me disappear forever over a vendetta I had nothing to do with. At this point, I figured he was going after me because he thought he could make it stick after my history of finding dead bodies, and he could hurt my whole family through one person.

"We need to look at this again. We have to make this make sense. I can't leave again until we do."

Dean had his phone in his hand and was typing out a message. I left him to it as I stood in front of the board and traced all the different avenues we'd looked into. Everyone in town seemed to love Emma, even Mrs. Lincoln. She was personable, happy, and good at what she did. She was also nice. So, who would want to kill her?

I kept going back to the cult aspect. She had been part of the cult, and Willow had been told she and her husband died when, in reality, they had left the cult. I assumed that was under the dark of night because everyone else seemed to think they were dead. And they'd made a life here for the last ten years where no one had bothered them. Where had they lived before that? Willow had said they'd left at least a decade before they came here, so why did they not have any info before they moved here?

But if someone had found them, if someone had happened upon them and they wanted to really make sure they were dead because they had up and left the ugly cult based on having the magic blood, but no access to the magic itself, then how was I ever going to find that person? Especially when the chief of our police was in on it somehow and wanted my blood for the punishment that had been meted out to his line?

My eye was drawn to the picture of the three trees. Why had Cypress been so angry when I mentioned Aspen and Willow? Sorrow, I would have expected, even regret. But anger? No. So then what else was there that would have made him angry?

Dean wrapped his arms around me from behind. "You want to tell me what happened now so that I can help?"

I laid it all out to him from the weird email that Cypress never actually got or that he was lying about getting, to the chief accosting me in the alley. Dean was about to burst through the door to go get him when I laid a hand on his arm.

"Are we making this too complicated?" I asked, staring at the board as a big picture instead of each individual piece. "I mean, we have the threats from Moron, of course, and the weird way I found Emma, but what if it's not that weird or doesn't have as much twistiness as we're trying to give it? What if Rick killed her? He's the husband, he had a girlfriend, he might have been making plans to leave, and instead of doing the divorce route, where he'd lose money by having to split things up, he took the murder route. He used to be in that cult, too. He could have known how to curse the chocolate, or he really could have just used one of the many chemicals in the flower shop to poison her, and then put in the call to Sharon that he was at the campground, and could she please have me pick up the flowers so I could find the dead body instead of him."

"You're not wrong, and that has a lot of possibilities. Plus, he ran when he saw Willow, so he wouldn't necessarily have any other motive than wanting to be done with his marriage without having to pay anything."

"True."

"And Aunt Hellen said she didn't like all the things that Rick had done, which made me think he might have been a shady character. Plus, Taboo growled when he saw Rick. It could have been because the dog watched the husband give the wife poison, then shut her in that big refrigerator and leave." He pointed to the picture of the chocolates. "He could have left those chocolates for you, knowing the chief would come looking for you because you were the last one in there. Not to mention, we can't be certain that he was actually at the campground when he said he was. He could have locked the door behind you from outside as he left and then driven to the campground so that his story had facts, just not in the time he'd said."

I moved to the many words I'd been given from the book with Poobah. "But how do all these connect then?"

"I'm not entirely sure, but it's not like every single thing we've ever found has been integral to the investigation. Maybe it's talking about something else?"

I didn't know if I could believe that, but I did know I wanted to talk with Rick without him running away. Now we just had to find him. Maybe I could put Isaac on tracking his phone or something else private eye-ish like that.

Ten minutes later, I knew I had been right to give it to the Boy Wonder of electronics. He was going to make an amazing detective someday. His father had better think twice before committing crimes anymore, even low-key ones.

"Rick is at the shop," I said to Dean once I got the text back from Isaac. "I bet he's cleaning things out so that he can get out of town now with as much as he can before they catch him."

"They're probably not looking for him since the chief is still set on you."

"Well, I'm looking for him, and that's enough." I shot back a huge thank you with some ridiculous emojis to Isaac's message, then realized I had missed a few texts from my mom with pictures of Amelia's river adventure, two from Anjanetta and her husband, and another from Mena saying she was out with Micah. Isaac sent back a smiley face smacking its head, and my job there was done.

"Off we go to Petal Paradise," I said, grabbing Dean's hand and practically dragging him with me. I was not doing this one by myself. Especially if the chief was still out in the alley.

As we walked to the car—I wasn't walking the whole way to the shop this time—I sent a text to Norm asking if the chief was back at the precinct. He shot back quickly that he was. That made me feel a little better, at least, although that was short-lived, because Sharon also texted me to let me know a check I had written to her had bounced and we needed to talk about it.

I sent that into the back of my mind. That was the least of my worries, although it was a worry. How was that possible? I'd paid her our final invoice to close out the job last week, but I hadn't looked to make sure that the check had cleared. It had to wait, though, because we had pulled up at the back of the flower shop, the scene of my latest chief interaction.

I shivered as we got out of the car, but I also reminded myself the chief was at the office and Isaac said Rick was here. I could do this, especially with Dean at my side.

We exited the car, and I wondered how we were going to get Rick's attention to come out here. The front of the shop had been dark, so he was most likely in the back, which was the reason we'd decided to come back here. There were several cars parked across from us, and I wasn't sure which was his, but Isaac had orders to let me know if he left.

"Should we knock?" I asked.

"Maybe it's open."

I shook my head at the ridiculousness of that possibility, only to watch the back door to Petal Paradise swing open inwardly on silent hinges. Wow.

Dean put his finger up to his lips to shush me, but I didn't need to be told, especially when I heard Rick talking.

Both Dean and I plastered ourselves on either side of the open door, just over the threshold, to get a better position to hear him clearly.

"I'm so happy you finally had time to talk. I think there are some very bad things going on, and I'm no longer sure that Emma actually died of natural causes." Rick was farther along in the shop. Was he talking on his cell phone or was there someone there with him?

We were about to find out. I swung the door almost closed behind us, leaving it open a crack just in case we had to make a quick getaway.

Chapter 26

There was no immediate answer, and Dean and I looked at each other with frowns. He must have been talking on the phone, which meant we weren't going to know who he was talking to unless he said the name.

But we assumed too quickly because suddenly there was another voice, and it was closer than Rick's.

"Of course, I'm here. I'll always be here for you. I told you that when we first started talking. As soon as you sell the shop, we can begin our life together in another city. I found a lovely place about two hours from here that would fit us perfectly." That was a voice I had spent hours and hours listening to over the phone, and in my inn, as we planned out the wedding that was going to be the start of my new life. What in the world?

"I'm sorry, Sharon, but I'm not going to be able to stay in the state. I just saw one of the people who I used to know when I lived in that..." He hesitated, and I wondered what he'd say next. "That group situation I told you a little about. And if she's in town, then there might be others, too. I told Emma all those years ago we should have moved several states over, and I'm not making that mistake again. We're going to have to look farther away. Think of it as a real fresh start. We can do some traveling and check out some spots. I don't have to be here to sell the shop, and I assure you I have enough with the life insurance that we'll be fine until we find somewhere we both love."

"But I love this place that's two hours away. And whoever you might have seen is probably long out of your 'situation,' as you call it. We can go be with my family now, and do all the things we've dreamed about." Sharon's voice was getting sharper. Why? And what family was she talking about? There were a lot of places you could travel to in two hours around here.

I glanced at Dean, but he was looking down the hallway. Was he thinking what I was thinking? That some people might consider a cult a family...

"Your family can come visit us when we find somewhere out of state, darling. I thought I'd be able to stay because the people I used to know hadn't come into town in years and years, but I saw Willow at the inn, and I nearly killed myself trying to get away from her. That tells me that I can't remain here now. I hope you understand."

"I don't understand. I thought you wanted to have a life with me. You said you wanted to be with me wherever I wanted to live, and I want to live two hours away. You promised." It was almost a whine, but something felt off about it.

"It's understandable that you're disappointed, sweetheart, but I'm going to have to put my foot down on this one. We have to be out of the state. We won't be hurting financially, and I'll feel much safer. It will be best for us. I promise."

"Your promises aren't worth anything," she said in a wobbly voice, followed by crying.

I so wished I could actually see them to get a sense of their body language. I was having a hard time imagining Sharon as a love interest for Rick, but what did I know?

"Oh, my love, don't cry. It will all work out."

And then Sharon started laughing in a horribly, nasty way. "I don't think you understand what you've been a part of here, *darling sweetheart*. Chief Morony is already on his way to pick Roxy up. None of his officers would have arrested her, so he's going after her himself. You were the backup fall guy, but since Morony is getting Roxy, I don't need you anymore."

"What?" Something struck a wall, or at least I hoped that crack was only against the wall. I jumped and started moving farther into the shop, but Dean stopped me with a hand on my shoulder and a shake of his head.

"This Willow you're talking about? I've heard of her, but she hasn't been in the 'group situation' in a lot of years. She thought you were dead, to be honest. I overheard their conversation at the inn right after you left because I followed you there, and she was stricken that you were still alive. You should have stayed around and talked with her. You might have learned a thing or two. But that's no matter now because we're about to get everything we need, and Morony is going to make it happen."

"Make what happen?"

"Our return to power. You were one of them for a whole lot of years, and I know your lineage. That's why I was willing to put aside my comfortable place in the group and step back out into this disgusting world to catch your attention. It wasn't hard to do, which is a horrible look for you. I will never understand why anyone thinks the person who cheated on their wife to be with you wouldn't then cheat on you, but it works in my favor this time." She laughed again. "You were so ready and willing, it was almost a pity to actually take you away from her. I should have let you stay and be miserable."

"What...what are you talking about?"

Oh, I could have probably told him, but I waited to see what she had to say to confirm my suspicions.

"This whole thing was a sham. The group is running out of money, and people aren't looking for anyone to buy curses and wishes from anymore. They just go online to any social media site, and they can pick up all the tips and tricks without paying a dime. We've been aware of Emma's good fortunes for some time. You didn't exactly do a very good job of changing your name and only moving a hundred miles away. You're right, you should have pushed for a different state."

"This can't be true."

"It most certainly is, and the leader wanted her money, along with bringing you back into the fold. He felt you were worth more alive than dead, since we wouldn't be able to get the money without it coming through you. So, I was sent to romance you away from her. At first, we figured the divorce settlement would be big enough, but then the leader's brother was able to get his hands on some very interesting information that made it far more lucrative to kill her and blame it on Roxy in order to have a bargaining chip to finally get our powers restored."

"The council would never do that."

"They will if we have their highest priestess."

This time, when I glanced at Dean, he was looking right at me. I was in no way the highest anything. Who would tell them that?

"Roxy is the highest priestess?"

"That's what I was told. And being able to help her with her wedding was the perfect way for me to get her where I needed her when I needed her there, while also destroying everything she loves at the same time. It might not be a direct hit to the ones who shamed us in the first place, but it will be when we're done. Just a little chocolate to set the trap and then making sure it all went according to plan, as it has."

Rick gasped. "No matter how much you and the chief think you planned the whole thing out, it won't work correctly."

"*Baby*, I told you exactly where she was going to be because someone contacted Willow's dad and set up a meeting with him to discuss things. Not that they got the real Jeff. But they didn't have to, did they? Not when I know his schedule and could make sure that Roxy was in the right place at the right time. Just like I did when I made sure Emma tried the chocolates that the group is particularly fond of."

Rick stammered before getting any coherent words out. "You didn't."

"Oh, my, yes, I did. And I'd do it again. Emma Aspen made quite the little fortune here, and we need that plus the life insurance to be able to continue to survive. They thought you'd probably fall for me since you had this boring life, and I was willing to sacrifice my time to snare you, not that it took much. Roxy is the cherry on top of the sundae because she and her family are the whole reason we can't do what we should be able to do, which is have power."

"But...I'd never seen you before you moved to town," Rick said, his voice rising with each word. "When did you get involved with the group? I would have recognized you."

"Like you did with Willow? Well, I'm a newer member and believe in every single thing they teach. My family was cut off, too, and there needs to be payment for that."

"This is not the way to go about it." He sounded sincere, but I wasn't going to believe anything from anyone on the other side of that door anymore.

"Sure, it is. And you're not without fault in this, darling. You did everything I said, from leaving the box of chocolates out for Roxy to giving those special chocolates to Emma before you supposedly left to go to the campground. It was all planned down to the second." She cackled again, and it was getting on my last nerve. I stepped away from the wall, but Dean held me off for a second time.

"Did you cut my fuel line at the campground, so I couldn't leave?"

"Didn't think I knew my way around a car, huh? I assure you I do. And it got you off the hook for the murder. You could at least thank me for that."

"I'm not going to thank you for anything. You killed her."

"Well, technically, she killed herself when she ate the chocolates you so nicely gave her. Which could mean you killed her. But it will never be that I killed her because I was the one who poisoned them. They can't and won't prove that. Not with Morony in charge. He wants Roxy, and I'm going to give her to him. Your part in this is done."

"No matter what you do, no one is going to believe that Roxy killed Emma. Her family loved my wife. They're taking care of our dog. They made sure to leave a tip on the counter after having to pick up their own flowers. What evidence does Morony even have? Nothing will make this right."

"We'll see about that." Her voice had dropped to a kind of purr that I'd heard in many a thriller right before bad things happened. "Why don't you just take this chocolate, like a good boy?" she taunted. "It will help you think while we come up with a plan that will make the case against that irritating bridezilla that no one can crack."

Rick. Rick was standing on the other side of the door talking with Sharon. Sharon, who had come highly recommended by Emma. Sharon, who had texted me, distraught that her friend had been killed, and was asking that I look into things to make absolutely certain that the right person was arrested, because she knew it couldn't be me.

And yet, it sounded like she had set it all up between herself, the chief, and Rick, even if he hadn't been aware of the lengths they were willing to go to make sure that I was the one who got put away for something that I didn't do.

"Although the more I think about it, maybe I don't need to share with anyone. If you hadn't been such an incompetent fool and just left the door unlocked behind her when she was in the flower shop the first time, then we could have kept it simple. In fact, we could have left it as Emma had a heart attack and died right there in the place she loved above all else. But no, Morony wanted Roxy to be the bad guy because her family is horrible."

"You can't do this." Something—Rick's fist?—banged on the wall.

"I'm not stupid, Rick, and neither is Morony. It made sense that since she had found the other three dead people, casting suspicion on her wouldn't be out of character, especially since Norm has been after her every time about putting her nose in things she shouldn't. We'll just make it true this time."

"You've lied to me all along. I thought we were just leaving Emma behind, not killing her." His voice was pleading, and I so wished I had the ability to read people's minds.

I did have the ability to use the book in my hand, though. I just really hoped it wasn't going to flare with light that they'd be able to see down the length of the hallway.

What do I need to know about this pairing? I thought and flipped the book open. Instead of the words sparkling or rising out of the book, they scrambled themselves on the page, kind of like what the puzzle had done.

Beware, she who seeks to *ruin* a *marriage* for *fortune* by *dating* and demolishing. *Secrets* will lead to unmasking this *creature.* Keep *close* to *crowded* areas of *light* for *renewal* and *justice.*

Well then. All I needed was for someone to make me happy and green—maybe a Kermit costume was in my future?—and I would have all the words from that freaky puzzle.

Unfortunately, because I was distracted with my brain scrambling facts, thoughts, and clues, I didn't keep myself from gasping as those dots connected like the outline of the murderer standing down the hall.

And that gasp caused the two people we'd been eavesdropping on to both poke their heads around the doorway where they were talking, leaving me face to face with Rick and Sharon. Uh oh.

"You!" she shouted as she reached into her bag.

Rick started stumbling over his words. I couldn't make out what he was saying because I was paying too much attention to the fact that Sharon had a knife in one hand and a box of chocolates in the other.

Chapter 27

I was so shocked at the absolute hate gleaming in Sharon's eyes that at first I didn't understand the sound I heard. It was like a yell, but also a groan. It took me off guard, almost as much as when the exterior door swung hard inward and totally smashed into Dean, sending him into the wall and pinning him there.

And in the doorway stood Cypress, former cult member, current father to Willow, and grandfather to two of the most amazing children I had ever had the pleasure of spending time with. And he was holding a gun, which, in my opinion, totally out-lethaled whatever Sharon had at her disposal.

The question top-most in my mind, though, was who would he aim it at? Me for blinding him with a book and making a whole bookshelf of files fall on him? Or Sharon for being a part of a group he had sacrificed everything to get out of, including his daughter and the future she had made for herself? A group that had killed a wonderful woman and tried to get away with it simply because they were greedy and had wanted her money.

"Sharon, why don't you come on over here? I have a proposition for you that I think you'd be very interested in hearing." He was a tall man, and a good-looking one, and I had never in my life wanted so badly to wipe the roughest floor in the world with someone's face.

"Jeff, what are you doing here?" she asked, still holding her box of chocolates and her wicked-looking knife.

"Like I said, proposition." He shrugged, but did not lower the gun. "I have what you deserve, and in fact, I also have an in to get that very same thing for you."

Her eyebrows pulled down, and she lowered the knife slightly. "What do you mean?"

He kept the gun straight and steady with one hand and with the other he snapped his fingers. A tiny flame ignited on his pointer finger then danced its way to his middle finger, across to his ring finger, landing on his pinky finger next. Finally, he turned his palm up, and the entire thing held a magnificent and spellbinding ball of blue, white, red, yellow, and orange that was so intense I would have covered my eyes if I didn't think I would get shot for moving.

The flaming ball undulated, and I finally had to look away because there was a hypnotic quality to it that I did not want to get lulled into acquiescence by.

But Sharon and Rick did not look away, and Dean was still pinned against the wall by the door.

"Now, about that proposition," Cypress said. "You'll want to drop whatever you have in your hands right onto the floor, then kick it over my way. That's right," he said as Sharon dropped the knife and the box of chocolates by simply unclenching her fingers. She soccer kicked them toward him a second after they hit the ground. Rick looked a little less sure of himself since he had nothing to drop, but he still opened his hands and pointed his fingers toward the ground as if dropping something, even though he had nothing.

"Good job. Now, you're going to call this Moron and let him know that you've accomplished your mission, but you need him to come over this way before getting Roxy. It'll be important for him to meet you here because you have very solid evidence he's going to want to collect before he visits the inn. You understand how important the evidence is?" he asked.

Rick nodded and fumbled his phone out of his pocket. Sharon, though, kept her eyes steady on Cypress. "I can have what I want?" she asked in a monotone.

"Everything you deserve will be yours. Make the call, Sharon, and everything you deserve will be yours."

I could see and hear the trap he was setting, and I let it roll. It was manipulation that would ultimately hurt her, which Cypress might have to pay a price for, but it was his choice, and I certainly wasn't going to stop him if it got all the bad actors in the same place at the same time. It was obvious he wasn't on their side in this, and I only hoped he wouldn't leave before talking with Willow, as I'd asked her not to leave without talking to her own child.

I slowly withdrew my phone from my pocket and texted Norm to get over here as soon as possible and to bring anyone he thought he might need to arrest three people, including his own chief.

I didn't know if he meant to or not, but he sent me a thumbs-up emoji, and I couldn't help but think how fitting.

***

I had promised Glennis the week off after the wedding because I knew how much she was in charge of with the rehearsal dinner, the lunch for the wedding itself, that amazing red velvet cake she had made, and brunch the next day. Then I'd added to that with the breakfast once Willow had come home.

There was much debate in the car if I should call her or just text her about making dinner tonight so that Cypress could join us. Dean thought I should just text her, but I was leaning more toward a call.

"I just think calling will make her hear my voice and not sit there and debate on how to type out telling me no. She loves to cook, and I'll give her an extra day off another day. She's always got something in the freezer that she can make. I'd do it myself if I didn't think I had already tested the limits of good things happening in one day."

"You could always see if you could get Mena to talk her into it, though, I think maybe Cypress has the market cornered on the manipulation thing. I can't believe he got Sharon to call Morony and have him come down and bring his notebook of supposed evidence with him. I've never been so satisfied to see someone perp walked away. And Rick's not going to get off scot-free either. That was awesome," Dean said.

And it had been. Grady Morony had come flying around the corner into the alley only to be met by our entire police force, out and guns drawn. Our lovely mayor had stood in the middle of the whole force and personally put the cuffs on Moron, reading him his Miranda rights as he balked, yelled, and promised revenge.

I ignored him because I had made one call already, and that was to the high council, who had not been aware that a sect of those with the blood, but without the talent, had formed their own council. They were handling that right now, and then we had a meeting scheduled next week to talk about some issues I thought were long overdue to discuss. We'd see what happened.

But first, we had a dinner that I had to convince Glennis she wanted to cook. I could have just gotten strombolis again, but I wanted special food for this one, and Glennis was the only one who could make the special-est of food. It was her own brand of magic.

As soon as we parked, I got out of the car and made my way toward the kitchen. Maybe if I did a quick inventory of the walk-in refrigerator and freezer, I could have a battle plan on how to convince her how easy it would be to just come on over and throw a few things together.

Except that when I pushed open the door to the kitchen, it was a hive of activity.

"You just turn yourself right on around and head back into your territory, young lady," Glennis said with a huge butcher knife in her right hand. "I've got this covered, menu's all set, and your red velvet cake is going in the oven as we speak. Be ready in an hour to eat, and do not make me ring the dinner bell again."

All I did was salute her and turn myself around to head back to the murder board room, where I found Poobah napping on the couch with Taboo sprawled out on the floor next to him. Poobah's hand was draped over the edge of the couch and rested on the dog's head. Moose had taken up a post on Taboo's chest, and Daffy was curled into his armpit.

I quietly backed out. I could pull down all the info later. It could wait while they slept.

Backing out into the hall, I bumped into Dean.

He twirled me around and then held me tight. "Good job today, but let's not do that anymore."

"Deal. The only mystery we have left to solve then is what was with the green and the happy on that puzzle."

"Well, the green could be all the money that Rick is not getting, and the happy could be us."

"True, but then why have it rise out of the book when the rest had to do with the evil of Sharon?"

"Or was it an opportunity for Cypress to redeem himself?"

"I know! I know!" Amelia yelled from the lobby. I quickly walked down the hallway toward her so that we didn't wake Poobah and his menagerie.

"You know what?" I asked.

"I know who had the answer to that."

Dean and I both looked at her, waiting for her to tell us, but apparently, we needed to actually ask. This child.

"And who has the answer to that?" I finally said.

"The nines lady. She knows all kinds of stuff, and she said that she watches over all of us, even the ones who don't think they need any kind of protection."

"The nines lady?" Dean looked as confused as I was until I remembered Earl having talked about the number that Amelia was listening to old-time music through. Had someone actually been talking to her, and we didn't know it? I was so happy to have had some of that happiness, and now I was going to turn green in the face from feeling sick to my stomach. Great.

Before I got out ahead of myself, though, I decided to do a quick bit of investigation. It was easy enough to open the door to the phone booth under the stairs and step in. I picked up the receiver and dialed three nines, then waited while the line rang and rang. I was about to hang up when finally there was a click, and old-time music sounded through the phone as if from far away.

"Hello? Who is this? Where are you?" I said. I waited a bit and tried again. "I have a bunch of people in this very house that could pull you out of wherever you are and make your life, or afterlife, or both, very miserable if you don't tell me who you are. You do not mess with my family and then hide. I won't allow it."

"There she is," a cultured and very feminine voice said on the other end of the line. "My darling descendant, you are one of the most special people in my world, and I am so happy to finally be able to talk to you. I was green with envy when I saw that you have mastered our shared talent in a way I was never able to."

"Our...descendent...special...envy..." It was like my brain had stopped cooperating with my mouth. Was this my ultimate grandmother?

"We'll have plenty of time to talk in the future, my darling Roxanne. There are many things that I'd love to tell you, but first, I need a favor for a friend. Something you can do for your greatest grandmother."

It had to be her. Holy wow, I was talking with my ultimate great-grandmother, Mary Margaret, who had pulled into this landing many years ago instead of traveling the rest of the way to Harrisburg. She'd chosen to remain here instead of submitting to an arranged marriage that would have taken away all of her powers, but could have made her one of the richest people on the East Coast. Instead, she'd made a life here with a man who had fallen in love with her, and together they'd put together this inn and started the very long line that led to my sisters and me.

I had so many questions!

"Anything," I said softly and with awe.

"I need you to go let Earl into the room at the end of the hallway in the basement. He's waited a long time to be able to do this, and finally, he's ready. We'll talk again soon. I'm so proud of you, all of you, and you are everything I could have dreamed of and more when I got off that ship."

And then she hung up on me. I was stunned enough to still be holding the phone in one hand and bracing myself against the wall with the other when Dean came into the small, cramped space.

"You okay?" he asked. "I heard your voice, but not the words, then you went silent and didn't come out."

"I'm...well...I'm a lot of things right now, but the top priority is apparently I'm also a doorman or door lady, as the case may be."

I had so much more to say, but first, Dean and I were on a mission.

We didn't tell anyone where we were going after sending Amelia back to her mom, who was talking quietly in the library with her father, before the dinner, where we'd all sit and hopefully no one would throw any bread. My grandmother gave me a set of instructions, and I retrieved a key from the back of the puzzle closet that my grandmother had directed me to, and then we went down the stairs into the basement.

Not surprisingly, I found Earl pacing in front of the door. I still couldn't tell you if it had always been there. But it was there now, and I had the key to unlock it.

"Earl," I said.

He raised his head, and his eyes looked bloodshot, his hair was tousled, and his sleeve hung down over his hand because it had come unbuttoned. "The room is calling me," he said in a monotone.

"I have the key." I held it up and hoped with everything in me that it was on the happy side of things, even though it had been created by the woman he had tried to kill when he couldn't control her.

Inserting the key into the lock, I turned the knob and then gently swung the door open.

Earl floated through the opening and then stood in the middle of the floor, rooted to the spot, as if he had been planted there. I didn't know where to look first, and I was pretty sure he didn't either. Every wall and the ceiling were covered in pictures and small, short videos showing him helping people with or without their knowledge. Some were old enough that there was no way a moving picture would have been available at that time, and yet they played over and over again. Earl was helping someone who was drowning in the river. Earl was catching a child who had stumbled down the stairs from the second floor and planting him on that third step from the landing softly, so he didn't fall. Earl was pulling the fire alarm when the kitchen had been on fire in what looked like the really early 1900s.

So many instances when the person he helped had no idea how they'd survived, but were so grateful they had.

And every single one had Earl at the center as the hero.

"Not a hero," Earl said at my elbow. "I did it because I was looking for redemption, and yet, when I finally did let the light take me, it was not to Heaven, and so I begged for the chance to come back here, not only to save you, but to also at least partially save myself from burning for eternity."

"I'm glad you came back," I said. "And I'm sorry that you were going to burn, hopefully this basement is at least a little better than Hell, right? Cooler anyway."

He actually laughed out loud, and a glow formed in the doorway. I turned around, and even though I'd never seen her before, except in a few pictures and a painting, I knew without a shadow of a doubt that I was standing in the presence of Mary Margaret.

"It's about damn time," she said with the same voice as she had on the phone.

Earl plastered himself to the wall behind him and bowed his head.

"Oh, don't even do that. You've been ready for this for many, many years, but have been too stubborn to actually ask. I should have known it would take someone like Roxy to make you finally start seeing yourself as we all have for decades."

"What do you mean?" he asked in a soft voice.

"I mean that you redeemed yourself time and time again. You were never asked to do any of these things. You took them upon yourself. No one does the right thing all the time, and you chose a doozy to make a wrong decision on, but in the end, you deserve peace, and this is that peace. It's yours, all you have to do is take it."

Removing the key from my hand, she thrust it at Earl, but he stuck his hands behind his back. "I don't want it. I want this. I want to be here, doing all the talking with Amelia, and watching Roxy and Dean grow. This is my family now, and I want to be a part of it."

"Even better," she said, snapping her fingers, and then the key was gone, but the scenes kept playing. "I'll be around if you need me for anything, and we'll talk later, Roxanne. Right now, I hear feet running on the floorboards, and the door is about to burst open. Go celebrate the next best day of your life, and may every day be better."

I wasn't going to go against those marching orders. I had lasagna to eat and red velvet cake to consider sharing, if I was so inclined. And a life to make with all the various parts and pieces of my heart that existed outside my body in the form of my family and friends.

Sure enough, the door whipped open at the top of the stairs, and Amelia yelled down that Isaac had found a new case that we might want to look into, and Micah could help if he'd stop making googly eyes at Aunt Mena. She was going to go tell Didi and Bopper that dinner was almost ready.

All I did was kiss Dean, and knew that, no matter what came next, this was home.

Check out these other mysteries from Rowan Prose:

Misty Simon, who also writes as Gabby Allan, always wanted to be a storyteller. Today, she has more than 30 titles to date in the romance and mystery genres. She lives with her husband in Central Pennsylvania where she is hard at work on her next novel or three.
www.mistysimon.wordpress.com

www.ingramcontent.com/pod-product-compliance
Lightning Source LLC
LaVergne TN
LVHW040138080526
838202LV00042B/2945